More praise for Lydia Adamson's
Alice Nestleton Mysteries

"Witty . . . slyly captivating."   —*Publishers Weekly*

"Another gem for cat mystery fans."
    —*Library Journal*

"Cat lovers will no doubt exult . . . charming
sketches of the species."   —*Kirkus Reviews*

"A blend of the sublime with a tinge of suspense
as Alice, like her four-pawed friends, uses her
uncanny intuition to solve a baffling mystery."
    —*Mystery Reviews*

"Whimsical. Lifts readers out of the doldrums
with cheery characters who steal the show."
    —*Midwest Book Review*

"Highly recommended."   —*I Love a Mystery*

"An ideal stocking stuffer for cat-doting mystery
fans."   —*Roanoke Times* (VA)

"Cleverly written, suspenseful . . . the perfect gift
for the cat lover."   —*Lake Worth Herald*

Other Books in the Alice Nestleton Mystery Series

A Cat
with No Clue

An Alice Nestleton Mystery

Lydia Adamson

A SIGNET BOOK

SIGNET
Published by New American Library, a division of
Penguin Putnam Inc., 375 Hudson Street,
New York, New York 10014, U.S.A.
Penguin Books Ltd, 80 Strand,
London WC2R ORL, England
Penguin Books Australia Ltd, Ringwood,
Victoria, Australia
Penguin Books Canada Ltd, 10 Alcorn Avenue,
Toronto, Ontario, Canada M4V 3B2
Penguin Books (N.Z.) Ltd, 182–190 Wairau Road,
Auckland 10, New Zealand

Penguin Books Ltd, Registered Offices:
Harmondsworth, Middlesex, England

First published by Signet, an imprint of New American Library,
a division of Penguin Putnam Inc.

First Printing, December 2001
10 9 8 7 6 5 4 3 2 1

Chapter 1

Alexander Woodward and Lila Huggins.

Do the names ring a bell?

You surely know of Burns and Allen, Eli Wallach and Anne Jackson, Lunt and Fontaine, Hume Cronyn and Jessica Tandy—to name just a few famous theatrical couples.

But Woodward and Huggins? Maybe not. Probably not.

I, however, know them and revere them. From the 1950s through the mid-1980s, they were brilliant character actors. Alone or together, they graced a hundred stages.

Their specialty was the bit parts in the imported productions—Ibsen, Chekhov, Racine, et al.—that usually ran five weeks and then bye-bye.

But their fame in the theater world comes not from their acting. Not at all. They are known because they are the proprietors of a quirky little restaurant, the Red Witch, on the second floor of a rickety building on West 3rd Street, in Greenwich Village. Alex and Lila started it in the 1960s because they were starving. Acting work was, to say the least, scarce. The restaurant quickly became, and remains, a place where out-of-work actors and not a few celebrities are compelled to visit for companionship, adulation, criticism, and cheap meals.

The Red Witch is unusual in several ways. You can get coffee and snacks all day long, but real meals are only served from about 10 P.M. until 3 A.M.

And because Alex and Lila run the Red Witch like a repertory company, the quality of the meals varies wildly. A chef rarely stays on for more than three months. Some of these chefs are world class, some right out of cooking school.

The cuisine is as diverse as the quality. Early American. French. Senegalese. Jewish. Italian. American Indian. Afghani. Hungarian. To name but a few.

One of the more endearing aspects of the Red Witch is the fact that no two table settings are alike. The two starving actors outfitted the place one chair, one cup, one spoon at a time.

One of the less endearing aspects is the fact that the walls are lined with huge blowups of still photographs from the horrendous movie called *The Wake of the Red Witch*, a Hollywood seafaring extravaganza, circa 1950, which starred, among others, Gail Russell.

Why did they decorate the restaurant with those photos? I never found out. Maybe Alex and Lila found them in a dumpster somewhere.

Or maybe it was just a kind of national eccentricity. After all, Alex and Lila are both English born, even though, in a profound sense, New York City bred.

I love them dearly, which is why I was trudging through the dirty snow, making my way to their apartment on that cold Sunday afternoon in February.

On this day every year their friends troop over to their West 57th Street digs—never to the Red Witch—to have coffee with them. Stale cookies are also provided.

It is the annual wedding anniversary celebration of Lila and Alex. This year, number fifty-five and counting.

No gifts brought, no alcohol served. Just a little get-together. And no one stays for very long. When I first started attending these gatherings, about eighteen years ago, there were wall-to-wall people. Death and relocation—but chiefly death—have thinned the crowd out over the years.

They live in an old red-stone building between Ninth and Tenth Avenues, way up on the fifth floor. There is no elevator. Alex claims that fifty percent of all climbs up result in his collapse on the second landing, where he lies unconscious for an hour and is then kicked back down the stairs by an unfriendly neighbor. Alexander has a rather macabre sense of humor.

I arrived at two-forty, was buzzed in, climbed up the five flights, and knocked on their door.

A stunning young woman answered. Forest-green eyes, long black hair that fell every which way, and the body of a stripper. She was wearing spiked heels, tight overalls, a black velvet sweater, and a scarf at her neck.

I didn't know who she was. But I did intuit what she was.

In addition to hiring theater people for the restaurant, Alexander and Lila always provided room and board for out-of-work, out-of-rent actresses. Sometimes they stayed only a few days, sometimes it was weeks, and in a few instances it was much longer than that—even as long as two years. While these young women lived in the apartment, Lila characterized them as her secretaries, and they did everything from cooking and cleaning to—well, to being secretaries.

"I'm Asha," the creature declared. Then, in response to hearing my name, "Are you *the* Alice?"

"Well, I am Alice Nestleton."

"Good! Excellent! Lila has been waiting for you."

Really? I thought. Why?

Asha led me into the sprawling apartment with its beautiful wooden floors, high ceilings, and twisty hallways. The building had once been a mansion, and

4

even after having been cut up, divided, subdivided, and degraded over the years, the apartments were still magnificent.

Passing through the living room, I saw the small circle of guests surrounding the seated Alexander, who was holding court as usual.

I spotted a photographer I knew—Brad Carmody.

And a musician named Lister.

And the baker Nozak, who supplied the Red Witch with breads and pastries.

Asha led me to the study and vanished after she ushered me in.

I had been in this room before. Nothing but four walls of bookcases, two large easy chairs at opposite ends of the room, and a very thick rug.

"My dear Alice! You always look so splendid in the cold weather. I do believe you are that rarest of creatures—a winter woman. Of course, if I recall, you are from the harsh climate of North Dakota."

"Minnesota," I corrected her, laughing. She looked good. Rather, she looked no older or wearier than she had last year.

"Do you find it peculiar that I am lying on the floor, Alice?"

Actually she was sitting on the rug, legs extended at arthritic angles.

What I did find "peculiar" was that she was wearing pajamas.

"Sit down. Join me," she said, patting the rug.

"I thought I would just say hello to Alexander first. Then I'll come back," I said. I really did not care to sprawl out on the floor, truth be told.

"But you'll miss the floor show," she moaned.

"What floor show?"

"Just come down here beside me for a minute."

I lowered myself onto the rug, not a little annoyed.

Suddenly, from the back of one of the chairs, came two little cannonballs, hurtling toward me.

One tumbled and rolled over, then quickly recovered and joined the other.

A second later, two adorable orange tabby kittens were sliding up and down my arms and legs.

"Alice, I want you to meet Billy and Bob. Don't ask me which is which."

"When did you get them?" I asked in delight.

"A few days ago."

"*Where* did you get them?"

"Oh, I have my sources," she said.

The kittens had another burst of energy, then jumped off me and collapsed, as kittens will. I watched them as they snoozed.

"I spend hours with them," Lila admitted. "Alex thinks I've gone around the bend."

"Doesn't he like cats?"

"Grudgingly, Alice. He says he gets exhausted watching them. He says they remind him of Bob Fosse. You do know Bob Fosse, don't you, dear?"

"Yes, sure. Although I never worked with him. Besides, Lila, he's dead. For some years now."

She cocked her head and appeared to be contemplating something I had said. Then she began slowly to get to her feet. "Come. Let us join the crowd."

We slipped out of the room, closing the door softly behind us, and walked into the living room.

Alexander was still addressing his subjects. Lila walked to his chair and sat on its arm.

She kissed him lovingly on the top of his head.

It was a simple, natural gesture . . . so common . . . seemingly without passion or importance . . . or anything.

It was just a mundane expression of friendship and intimacy between people who had lived together a very long time, in bad times and good.

No one in the room gave a second thought to that kiss.

Except me.

It jolted me severely, in head and heart.

It filled me with longing and dread.

Longing? Yes! Because in a sense that was what I craved . . . that was the relationship I had always craved with a man.

Dread? Yes! Because it dawned on me right there and then that I would never have it.

Surely not soon.

My man troubles had escalated to such an extent that I had decided on a temporary refuge: chastity.

My long-time lover, Tony Basillio, and I were now just friends.

My last extra-Basillio affair—the gentleman in question was one A.G. Roth—was passionate but brief. Upon termination it had also transformed into a curious kind of friendship.

I was very close to mawkish tears.

Alexander had now moved into his story of "nuptial origins," as he put it.

I had heard it before. At least eighteen times before.

In fact I knew it by heart. But, like the others, I listened, because, as critics used to say, "Alexander Woodward could make the telephone book sound like *Othello*."

The time is the 1940s. They are both young, English, and in New York, but they do not know each other.

They both get bit parts in a G. B. Shaw play.

Alexander falls head over heels in love with her.

She finds him obnoxious.

To entice her to his apartment he claims to be a great chef, and the son of a great chef. He invites her to dinner again and again. Again and again she refuses.

Finally she relents, and shows up with a friend.

Alexander, in fact, can cook only four things: omelets; mushrooms friend in butter and topped with sour cream; flank steak with onions; tapioca pudding.

He decides against the omelets and prepares the other three dishes for his guests.

At the end of the dinner, Lila announces it was one of the five worst meals of her life.

But she adds the dictum: "Any man who cooks so hard and so badly must have a heart of pure gold."

The story, once finished, was greeted with applause, as always.

I stayed for another half hour chatting with the others and revisiting the kittens.

Then I said good-bye to Alex and Lila, promising to visit the kittens often.

Outside, despite the powerful sun, the cold wind was whipping up litter.

I felt wonderful, my brief bout of tears aside. I always felt good after my visits to that couple.

I started walking east on Fifty-seventh, into the wind.

Half a block later, the wildest and most delicious idea surfaced.

It was a non-Nestletonian idea, to be sure, and it would never have occurred to me had I not been relatively affluent at the time.

Let me explain:

I had just completed work on a pilot for an independent TV producer who was trying to sell a series to the networks. It was a cop show—aren't they all. But with a difference. The producer figured that in a market saturated with such shows he would go back in time and do a "Broadway beat" cop show, situated in the 1950s. The series would be called "Broadway: Bad & Beautiful."

I played—would you believe it—a world-weary actress turned bartender!

Only a bit, of course, but I was $5,000 richer than I'd been last week.

So, my idea was simple. A gift for a wonderful old theatrical couple. No one had ever been allowed to bring them an anniversary present; they forbade it.

But this gift they would accept. How could they not?

I would send them a replica of the meal that eventually led to the nuptials. My friend Nora's restaurant, the Pal Joey Bistro, was only a few blocks away. I was so happy at conceiving the idea that I virtually skipped all the way there.

Nora didn't have any time for me. A tour group was booked in for late brunch. But I pulled her aside for a moment and asked for help.

Could her chef prepare mushrooms fried in butter and topped with sour cream, flank steak with onions, and tapioca pudding?

Could she have it delivered in an hour or two?

My friend Nora looked at me as if I were demented.

"Who would eat such a mess?" she asked.

"Eighty-five-year-old lovebirds."

Chaos was erupting all around us. Nora's staff was just not used to serving a full contingent for Sunday brunch.

"Okay, okay," she said. She pulled me to the bar and thrust a pencil and pad into my hand. "Write it all down, Alice. The dishes. The name and address."

"I am going to pay for this, Nora."

"Damn right you are. Plus a ten-dollar delivery charge. And if my chef quits over this order, you'll pay damages also."

Then she grinned, kissed me on the cheek, and rushed back into the fray.

She stopped in her tracks suddenly, turned, and asked, "Are you serious? Tapioca?"

"Yes."

"You poor child," she said, and fled.

I went home, still high from my brilliant idea. I went to a French movie staring a favorite actor of mine: Michel Piccoli. An old man now, but still a wonderful presence. But my, has he gotten fat.

I ate alone in a Moroccan restaurant on Bedford Street. It was delicious, except for the amorous waiter.

When I got back home, I brushed my Maine coon cat, Bushy, and tried to do the same for Pancho, the crazy one. No luck.

The phone rang at 10:14. For some reason I noted the exact time.

Lila Huggins was on the other end of the line. She was bubbling over with joy.

"We have eaten every scrap of that horrendous meal, Alice. It was the sweetest gift we have ever received from anyone. Bless you, dear. Alex sends his love. And so do Billy and Bob."

With that, she hung up.

I had never been happier in my life.

Then things turned, to use Lila's word, peculiar.

Exactly twelve hours later, meaning at 10:14 A.M. on the following day, I received a call from someone identifying herself as Asha.

She was hysterical.

It took me a few minutes to remember who she was.

She was calling from Roosevelt Hospital, she said. Both Lila Huggins and Alexander Woodward had been taken to the emergency room at eleven o'clock the previous evening.

Lila had died at seven in the morning.

Alex was still alive, but critically ill and in intensive care.

Asha hung up. I sat there, dazed.

Ten minutes later, there was another phone call from another hysterical woman.

Nora.

It seemed that one of her waiters had stepped out for a smoke at two in the morning and a lunatic waiting in the alley had pumped five bullets into his head.

Odder still was the fact that the murdered waiter was the one who had delivered the anniversary meal to Lila and Alexander.

Chapter 2

It was the first time a search warrant had ever been executed in the Nestleton compound. You can imagine poor Bushy and Pancho's shock as the searchers trooped in, accompanied by two homicide detectives, Fontana and Greco, the latter holding the paper high.

They were searching for the .25-caliber Beretta that murdered Nora's waiter. And for the stash of crystal methamphetamine, part of which had been used to murder Lila and cripple Alex.

This drug, dissolved in liquid form, had, according to their forensics, been mixed into the sour cream and mushroom dish, causing severe arrhythmia in the old couple—resulting in a massive fatal coronary for Lila and a disabling stroke for Alex.

To say that I was a suspect would be a severe understatement. As the questioning proceeded, it became apparent that the NYPD scenario put me in dead center.

As Detective Greco said: "From our point of view, the only thing you didn't do, Miss Nestleton, is mix the speed into the sour cream. Your partner Asha did this. But you ordered and orchestrated the meal. And you shot that waiter to death because he saw too much after he delivered the meal."

Can you imagine the stage set? A brooding West Side tenement in the dead of winter. The two detectives, me, and A.G. Roth seated around my long, rickety table. In the background the searchers poking, peeling, and penetrating. Bushy and Pancho on the window ledge, glaring.

Of course A.G. Roth was enjoying it all.

I had introduced him as my lawyer, which he wasn't. He was a theatrical lawyer. And the only thing he was really interested in at the time was the murder of Abraham Lincoln. Yes, that was A.G.—an obsessive hobbyist. In fact, he was currently tracking down a new conspiracy theory concerning Lincoln's murder, the focus being on one Sergeant Boston Corbett, the soldier who shot the fugitive assassin Booth to death before he could surrender and say a word. It seems Corbett ended up eleven years later in an insane asylum, from which he escaped and vanished forever.

Yes, A.G. is a bit peculiar. But at least he had shown up. I had called everyone after the tragedy—

only A.G. had wandered by to solace me. That is, I suppose, what ex-lovers are for. Besides, it was good to have him there; I liked looking at him. He was an attractive man, a bit too short, a bit too wide, but with one of those handsome, beat-up, middle-aged faces and the most casual way of wearing a business suit I had ever seen.

After Detective Greco laid out the main contours of the scenario, and the more elegant Detective Fontana affirmed his partner's wisdom with a constant refrain of "It makes sense, it makes sense"—you won't believe what A.G. said then: "You know, I have been acquainted with Alice Nestleton for some time now. And while I think she is capable of murder, a triple homicide is a bit excessive."

Thank you, counselor.

The two detectives looked at him as if he were crazy.

A.G. added, "Besides, she loved that old couple."

Greco ignored him and said to me: "You stated to us, Miss Nestleton, that after you ordered that meal in person, you went to the movies and ate dinner out, then returned home to your loft and remained here all night. You told us you did not go out again. Is that correct?"

"Yes."

"Was anyone with you in the loft?"

"No."

"Did you make any calls from here?"

"Not until morning. Lila called me to say how much she liked the meal, but that doesn't help us much."

"So no one can confirm your story?"

"Well," I said, pointing to the cats, "they can, I imagine."

Fontana guffawed. At that moment, dear old gray, half-tailed Pancho began one of his lunatic rushes and scared half to death a uniformed policewoman who was going through my laundry bag. Pancho then hurtled back across the loft and onto a kitchen cabinet, where he commenced to nap.

Detective Greco, who had a beautiful bristle haircut, making his head look like a carpet, asked, "Did you speak to the waiter Jerrard while ordering the food at your friend's café?"

"No."

"Have you ever spoken to him?"

"No. The only one I speak to in the Pal Joey Café is my friend Nora, the owner. And sometimes the bartender."

"Did you know Jerrard was going to deliver the meal?"

"No."

"Could you go over again the circumstances which led you to come up with that peculiar anniversary gift?"

I told them the whole story again. Then the contingent left. They had found neither weapon nor drugs.

A.G. and I remained seated at the table. Darkness flooded the loft.

"Should I turn on a light?" he asked.

"Do what you want."

The phone rang. It was Asha—my coconspirator, according to the police. Alex was dead.

The horrible consequences of my cute idea seemed to flood up out of my stomach and throat, like bad chile. I could scarcely breathe. Two people I had revered, and a young man I didn't even know, were all dead now because Alice Nestleton had a little money from a ridiculous acting job and a cute idea.

I laid my face down on the table.

"Do you remember the T-shirt kids used to wear?" A.G. asked.

I shook my head. I didn't know. I wasn't interested.

He took out a small pad and wrote something. He pushed a piece of paper in front of my face. It read: SHIT HAPPENS.

All I could say was, "Will you feed my cats for me?"

He nodded and walked away from the table.

Suddenly I was seized with an enormous rage. I stood up and screamed: "I'm going to do something about this! I am going to do something!"

"Yes, of course," he replied gently, and proceeded to deal with the small cans of turkey and rice.

Chapter 3

It was, to use that old rehearsal term, dicey, to bring together Sam Tully, A.G. Roth, Nora Kaye, and Tony Basillio in one space, even if it was my loft.

Basillio did not like Roth. He thought A.G. had alienated my affections for him. He couldn't understand that it was his enduring promiscuity with young actresses that had done the job.

Both Basillio and Roth did not like old Sam Tully, who had for so long dressed like a derelict that he had become one. And they had nothing but contempt for poor Sam's fiction effort—an attempt to resurrect his long-out-of-print mystery series featuring a crazed hard-boiled detective named Harry Bondo, the most famous title in that moribund series being *Only the Dead Wear Socks*.

Nora, on the other hand, was not bothered by either Roth or Sam, but she did not like Basillio one bit, primarily because she felt all stage designers were affected and megalomaniacal. This is understandable because Nora used to be in the musical theater.

But they all recognized that I was *in extremis,* and they behaved themselves, more or less, at least at the beginning of the meeting.

It became like a high school science lab. First there was a short lecture laying out the problem. I, of course, was the lecturer.

Then there was the lab work. Sam Tully filled the first test tube.

"The way I see it, honey, is that there are two, you hear me, only two legitimate suspects. One is that young bimbo Asha. Two is X—X being one of the guests who left the party late, after doping the sour cream. But, honey, believe me, the cops know this. They're on the case. So why don't you just relax and bake some bread."

He was wearing a ridiculous hat with earlaps, and he tugged at one lap while delivering his analysis. Then he popped one of the ultra cheddar chips I had provided for the group into his mouth and chewed. He longed for a little booze, I knew, but I had none. His predilection for morning drink had always appalled me. But the man was old; let him die inebriated. As Baudelaire said, the only good addictions are wine, virtue, and poetry. And Sam didn't have any of the last two that I knew of. So God bless him.

Then A.G. Roth noted: "If this was a plot in one of Sam's books, the great Bondo would have asked, 'What's the big deal? Any idiot knows that sour cream kills.'"

No one thought it funny. I glared at him.

Tony Basillio, that aging Lothario, leaned back on the chair, ran his hands through his hair as if to say, Look how thick my hair still is—and then patted his stomach as if to show me how flat and trim it still was, and then said: "The way I look at it, forget the killer for now. You have to look for motive. And what it looks like is that maybe sweet old Alex and Lila weren't the angels you thought they were. And maybe all kinds of bad things were going on in their sweet little restaurant."

"That's ridiculous!" Nora said, bridling at Tony's predilection to consider all restaurateurs illicit.

"Oh? Okay. Let's forget the Red Witch, Nora. How about your restaurant?"

"What are you talking about, you fool?"

"It appears to me that if one really wanted to name suspects, one would go right to your place, Nora. Either the chef or the dead waiter."

Nora was so enraged, she spoke through her teeth, real low. "Listen, you nitwit, poor Jerrard is dead, murdered. And my chef, Winston Plommer, is probably the kindest, finest man I have ever met in the restaurant business."

Tony chuckled cynically. Nora fumed more.

The matter then went to general discussion. After an hour of heated exchanges we had hammered out the parameters of our scientific inquiry. A simple three-pronged research project.

Investigate the Red Witch.

Look into whether Winston Plommer had any connection to the Red Witch.

Find out who Jim Jerrard really was.

As the meeting was disbanding, the phone rang. It was Asha. The moment I heard her voice again I cringed. Who else was dead?

But all she asked me in a plaintive voice was, "What do I do with the kittens?"

My God! I had forgotten all about Lila's kittens.

My guests were filing out the door. I scrutinized them intently for a possible caretaker. Nora hated cats. Tony still had the two Siamese I had forced on him. Sam had a crazy striped Bengal house cat who could not be socialized.

There was only one possibility.

So, to Asha, I said, "I'll be over shortly."

And to A.G. I said, "Don't leave yet. I have a delicious proposition for you."

He looked both hopeful and worried. Well he might.

Chapter 4

During the cab ride uptown I crushed A.G.'s opposition to his adopting the kittens.

I had a well-practiced, empirically proven method for bringing reluctant feline adopters around to reason. First I would explain how lonely and barren their life had become without a cat. Second I would say that this moment was fated—never had a human and a cat needed each other so much . . . and were so perfectly suited to each other . . . as if the very hand of Jehovah had reached down and plucked one cat and one human from the billions of possibilities and He said, "Lo, I have spoken. These two shall inhabit the same dwelling."

And finally I would reveal that there would be, alas, dire consequences if the potential adopter did not adopt. He or she would suddenly become prey to disease, famine, death, and all the horses of the apocalypse, including bankruptcy.

A reluctant adopter would also face a smaller hindrance, particularly if he was a male. It was revealed to me that he would soon inherit a mansion, and in that mansion would be fifty-five magnificent bedrooms, and in each room would be a beautiful bed, and in each bed would be a wild, gorgeous sex partner—but the reluctant adopter, it was revealed to me, would walk all night from room to room, bed to bed, partner to partner—both impotent and insomniac.

Yes, that is my usual method. With A.G., however, during that cab ride, I decided to use a simpler, less subtle method.

First I admired his old gunmetal-gray, wide-ribbed corduroy suit; then I kissed him, a kind of old-fashioned sexy kiss, a kiss that reeked of longing.

Then I whispered: "Surely, A.G., you'll take Lila's kittens until we find a permanent home for them."

He gave me a hurt look, as if asking, "What kind of fiend do you think I am that I would not provide sanctuary for such innocent creatures?"

And that was that.

Asha opened the door for us. She was no longer dressed flamboyantly. And her long black hair was pulled back into a bun. But she still took A.G.'s breath away.

A CAT WITH NO CLUE

I was about to quip, "Hello, sister killer," but I realized it was inappropriate.

Asha was in a bad state. The apartment was littered with cartons. The kittens were in an open suitcase, climbing in and out and back in again.

"Alex has a cousin in Toronto. He's coming here to liquidate everything. That's the word he used—liquidate. I wanted to tell him it has all been liquidated already." She laughed at her own bad joke, bitterly, then added: "So that's what I'm doing now. Getting everything in boxes."

"Well," I said, "you don't have to worry about the kittens. Mr. Roth will take them."

She nodded assent and continued her work. I had brought a large carrier. A.G. and I loaded the kittens into it, not without difficulty. A.G. seemed to be weakening in his resolve. I gave him a little subtle reinforcement.

Asha didn't seem to want to make conversation. What was there to say or do? Compare interrogations?

We started to leave.

Suddenly she shouted out: "What the hell am I supposed to do with this?"

She was holding up a single 8½×14 sheet of paper. She held it in one hand between thumb and first finger, as though it was infected.

"What is it?" I asked.

"It came in the mail a few days ago. It was sent to Lila. She said it was the stupidest thing she had ever seen or received."

"May I look?" I asked.

She brought the sheet of paper over to me.

What a peculiar document it was!

Essentially, a one-sided, rather primitive poster.

There was a headline in large bold type, obviously done by hand with a black magic marker.

It read:

FOUND!

THREE KITTENS ON WEST 54TH STREET!

CALL 897–3669.

And under the headline was an actual photo of three kittens.

Two of them looked exactly like Lila's little tabbies.

The third had the same body as the other two, but superimposed over its real face was the face of a gargoyle. A real ugly medieval gargoyle. A face half bat, half human. A forked serpent's tongue was thrusting out of its salacious jaws. A pair of jagged horns sprouted from the crown of its head.

I was confused. "Were the kittens ever lost?" I asked.

"Of course not."

"So why should it be sent to Lila?"

"Who knows! That's why Lila said it was stupid."

"Where did Lila get the kittens?"

"From a shelter in Queens. She saw them being offered on a cable TV station. They charged her fifty dollars for inoculations. And they brought the kittens to her."

"Can I keep this piece of paper?"

"Be my guest."

She closed the door behind us. A.G. started down the stairs with the carrier. I didn't follow him.

"What's the matter?"

The matter was the poster. I found myself staring at it. It was one of those infuriatingly absurd items that from time to time pop into one's life. I knew it meant nothing. At least I felt it was so bizarre, it had to mean nothing. There are more eccentrics in the West Fifties in Manhattan than any comparable place on earth. Maybe someone saw Lila years ago in a bit part that was irritating, and maybe that someone knew she had kittens, so she just created a lunatic poster and mailed it to poor old Lila. Who knew?

The gargoyle was the real kicker. That meant the sender was some kind of nut. But why superimpose a gargoyle on a kitten's face? Why not Marlene Dietrich or Madonna or Saddam Hussein or a milk cow?

The real kittens were starting to carry on in the carrier.

"Let's go," A.G. pleaded.

I folded the poster along the lines it had been

folded when originally inserted into the mailing envelope, and shoved it into my shoulder bag.

Then the door of Lila and Alex's apartment swung open. Asha appeared and said: "By the way, Lila called the number. It was a phone booth in Lincoln Center."

She closed the door. I followed A.G. and the kittens down the stairs. Down five long flights of stairs.

Chapter 5

It was evening when I returned to my loft. I had spent several hours in A.G.'s apartment on 12th Street and Fourth Avenue, clearing away the astonishing number of books and clippings pertaining to his latest passion—the Lincoln assassination—and setting up for him litter boxes, feeding bowls, and kitten accouterments.

When I did get home, Bushy was screeching and rambunctious. He didn't like to be kept waiting for the evening meal. He truly didn't. I threw a balled sock at him, cursed him for the Maine coon cat he was, and then, out of remorse, gave him a special treat—the dollar can.

As for Pancho, he couldn't have cared less about the evening meal, and I didn't have any of the delicacy he craved more than life itself—saffron rice, wet and warm, molded into a ball and plunked on top of his dry food. I often wondered what those pebbles tasted like. Maybe they were the feline equivalent of Shredded Wheat. I settled in for another brooding, festering night alone, the only kind I had experienced since that dreadful sour cream was consumed.

The phone rang at twenty minutes to eight. It was Detective Greco. There were some things to go over, he said. Your place or mine? The time: now. By his "place," I assumed he meant a precinct house. I was not interested. "By all means, come and have coffee with me," I replied.

They showed up very quickly. I didn't make coffee. Once inside, it was Detective Fontana who did most of the speaking. Perhaps they worked in shifts.

As I said earlier, he was an oddly elegant man. He wore an old-fashioned hat, perhaps felt. His suit was well fitted and the tie knotted with precision. He was tall and lanky and very fair haired and fair skinned, and because he was a bit stooped, he looked like a choir director about to start up the proceedings.

What quickly negated this gentle description was the constant peeking out from beneath his jacket of a large, ugly semiautomatic handgun in a kind of spring holster. I found it odd, sitting across from them, that they were smiling—but the smiles were definitely not comradely.

Anyway, the smile vanished from Fontana's face the moment he commenced the conversation. In fact, he pointed at me in a kind of *j'accuse* fashion.

"Why didn't you tell us you once worked for the NYPD?"

I was startled by the question.

"I really didn't work for you people," I protested.

"Weren't you a paid consultant for RETRO—a unit formed to go back over unsolved homicides?"

"Well, yes. But that was about ten years ago. And it was a very short-term contract. Ninety days, if I remember correctly."

"Why you?"

"You mean why did they take me on as a consultant?"

"Yes."

"It's all a bit hazy. It had something to do with a series of downtown murders. The victims all had cats. And the murderer left a cat toy at the scene of each crime."

"Did you clear the case?"

"The murderer was caught. Not by me alone. I did provide some help, I believe."

"You should have told us about RETRO."

"Yes. I'm sorry."

They exchanged a quick glance. I wondered if this meant that Greco would now replace Fontana as chief interrogator during this session, if this was indeed an interrogation. No. Fontana kept center stage.

"You're a very attractive woman," he said.

Hmm. What was going on now, over and beyond the arrogance of males?

"Actually," I replied flippantly, " I do believe you're correct. But I wasn't always so attractive. When I first came to New York I looked like one of those milk-fed blond bombshell Miss Americas who end up as Daisy Mae in a production of *Li'l Abner*. You know the type. It's nice to meet a man like yourself who realizes I'm so much more attractive now that I've aged a bit."

My tweaking of him made him a bit uncomfortable.

But he came back strong and a little bit out of character. "Why the hell didn't you tell us you're an actress? Maybe you forgot about RETRO, but you don't forget what you do."

"If I recall, Detective, you asked me during that first interview how I made a living. On an average, I now make more from cat-sitting than from acting. As difficult as that may be for you to believe. In fact, I am very much like what Alex and Lila were—bit players. With an occasional foray into good roles in obscure plays."

"I had a different take on your lie, Miss Nestleton. I thought you were trying to diminish your closeness with the victims. Maybe you were much closer than you let on. Like you kind of said—a kind of secret society of bit players."

I didn't answer for a long time. This man had unnerved me. He had hoisted me with my own petard. Was that the reason I loved Alex and Lila? Because I would be them eventually? Because we were on the same road . . . gypsies in a tent, mounting puppet shows in offbeat venues?

Sure, I had a few critical successes, a few meaty roles, but like it or not, I was a bit player. Oh, it was all getting so sad.

When I did speak, all I could say was: "It's late."

"Yes, we'll be leaving shortly. There's nothing much else to cover at this time, Miss Nestleton. Do you have anything you want to say to us? Maybe something that you forgot earlier? Any old thing would do."

"I can't think of anything."

The two detectives stood up and headed toward the door.

Greco turned back and called out: "By the way, I have regards for you."

"From whom?"

"Ed Lister."

"Who?"

"You have to stop playing us for fools, lady. You'll make us mean instead of the sweet cops we are now. Ed Lister was at the party. He was one of the last to leave. He told us he knows you. He told us you and him greeted each other."

Now I remembered the musician. We knew each other casually, very casually. He played piano for cabaret singers. I had met him because he once had a girlfriend who had been in a Dürrenmatt play with me.

"We didn't greet each other. We just made eye contact." It suddenly dawned on me that I had no idea why he was there. I had never seen him at such a party before. I never knew he was a friend of Alex and Lila, but the couple had always attracted diverse fans.

The officers walked out.

A bit shaken, I put on a Maria Callas CD, drank apple juice, ate stale crackers, and tried to make sense of the visit. They hadn't even mentioned the name Asha, which probably meant they no longer thought that Asha and I were working as a hit team. They had probably absolved her completely. Why not? The young woman was not stupid enough to kill in a manner, in a place, and at a time that left her as the most plausible murderer.

As for me, what did they really think? Probably that I knew a great deal more than I had told them . . . and that I had some twisted relationship with Lila and Alex over and beyond our theatrical bond.

I burst out laughing. Actually I knew less than I told them. And the only thing twisted about our relationship was an occasional mutual indulgence in licorice with Alex.

Chapter 6

Tony and I stood in front of the Red Witch. The red crayon sign on the door, pathetically printed in a childlike hand, read:

CLOSED IN LOVING MEMORY OF ALEX AND LILA

"There's someone inside," Basillio said, grabbing my arm for some reason.

He knocked.

Cynthia Quarles, the manager, opened the door. I had always liked this woman. About forty, she was tiny, and her movements were always jerky—but she exuded efficiency, was polite to everyone, and was the person who kept the restaurant afloat.

The moment she recognized me, she burst into tears. We blubbered together. Tony walked past us, into the restaurant, as if he were entering a beloved eatery. This was a fake entrance—an act. Most of the time Tony had refused to go there. He considered it a tourist place, which really was unfair of him. He disdained the Red Witch just because it had been listed in a few hip guide books as an "interesting little bistro with passable, inexpensive food, where theater people congregate at all hours."

The only thing he liked about the place was its dependence on a dumbwaiter to deliver the food from a subterranean kitchen to the second-floor dining area.

Cynthia led us to a table and brought us coffee—bitter black coffee and half-and-half in a pitcher.

She ran her hands over her short-cropped head, played with her ballpoint pen, and began to babble. I'd never seen her lose control like that.

"The police were here. Again and again. They never stop. Stupid questions. Did the restaurant have any trouble with suppliers? Did Lila and Alex owe anyone? Did they deal with bad people? For linens? For meat? For fish? Any disgruntled waiters or waitresses? Chefs? Did they catch anyone dipping into the till? Oh, they kept on going. They asked for a list of past and present employees. They asked for financial statements. And they wanted to know why we changed chefs so much. Why? Because we could never pay enough to keep a good chef. We get people to cook in the kitchen while they're looking for real work at a real restaurant that pays. When they find it, they're gone. The police couldn't understand that, and they couldn't understand that Alex and Lila didn't know anyone in the restaurant business who wasn't their friend."

"Did they ask you about Jim Jerrard?" I asked.

"Oh, yes. And about that chef, Plommer, from your friend's place. I never heard of either of them. I never heard Lila or Alex mention their names. And they never worked at the Red Witch. That's for sure."

The resident cat, Phoebe, sauntered by. Tony lowered the creamer.

"Please don't do that!" Cynthia said sharply.

Tony gave her one of his fake apologetic looks and replaced the little pitcher on the table. I noticed that the restaurant had several new tables; large butcher-block ones with crisp new red-and-white tablecloths. The specials board, which always hung over the dumbwaiter, was wiped clean. Why wouldn't it be? The restaurant was closed.

Cynthia fell silent. She put the ballpoint pen away and began to play with sugar packets. I felt a growing sense of desperation; if this woman knew nothing, no one knew anything.

I picked up one of the packets in a show, perhaps, of friendship, of solidarity, and I shook it. I said, "I didn't see you at the party."

"I was there. In and out a couple of times."

"Did you see anyone there who might harbor a grudge against Alex or Lila?"

"No. But most of those people are theater people, Alice. You know that. You know them better than me. But I'll tell you this: It was probably some crazy actor or director nursing a thirty-year-old grudge."

"What about Asha?"

"What about her! Lila gave her a job in the restaurant. Then took her in. Like she took in those damn kittens. Asha murdered them? Whoever thinks that is totally insane. And let me tell you something else, Alice. The police think you're involved."

"I know."

"So that's how crazy this thing is."

It was one o'clock when we left. I had called a meeting of the Nestleton Task Force for two-thirty that same day at a coffee shop on Church Street near Lispenard, the crossroads between Tribeca and Chinatown. Sam Tully wanted to meet at a bar. I didn't. I chose this place because it allowed smoking; Sam would not sit in a coffee shop that prohibited smoking. So there were not many options.

Tony and I arrived about one-forty-five. We ordered cappuccinos and waited. He started giving me his line . . . you know, how he misses me to death . . . how we ought to become lovers again . . . how we are and always have been and always will be closer than any two people on earth. Oh, yes, he had it honed to a fare-thee-well. I usually fell for it. But not this time. No, not at all. After his plea was finished we sat in silence.

Tully showed up at about two-ten; A.G. at two-twenty. Nora didn't show at all.

I called my machine. Yes, she had left a message. She couldn't make it. And A.G. had been a pain in the ass, she claimed. He had shown up to help her interrogate the chef. "What a stupid waste of time!" in her words. Plommer never knew who he was preparing that deadly dish for. And he'd never even heard of Alex and Lila or their restaurant. Nora's voice made it clear she was more than a bit perturbed.

I went back to the table. "Well, A.G., I see you followed up on that chef."

"Yes. I got zip on that front."

"So Nora told me."

"I got a whole lot more than zip," Sam blurted out, blowing a mammoth smoke ring skyward.

We waited for his explanation.

"The waiter who delivered the food—the one who got blown away, Jerrard—he was a comic. A bad one, I hear. Didn't work much. Played a club in Queens, over the bridge, in Long Island City. A topless comedy club. I spoke to the manager. A creep named Dallek. Guess what he told me."

When no one ventured a guess, Tully continued: "The kid was in to a very nasty loan shark for a whole lot of money. At least for him it was a whole lot of money."

Sam grinned, and slapped his hand down onto the table triumphantly.

"So you see what we got?" he asked.

"No," I replied.

"We got no connection at all between the murders. The shark just got tired of treading water. Boom! One dead debtor."

"Maybe," said Tony cynically.

"Maybe," I echoed.

A.G. didn't say a word.

"Well?" I demanded of him.

"Who cares?" he replied. "I have something of real importance."

Tony snapped at him. "You crazy? You just told us you came up with zip on Nora's chef."

"Tony has a point, A.G. Maybe Billy and Bob have deranged you. Kittens can be trying."

"Ah, trying they are," he agreed. Then his face lit up in a beatific smile. He asked: "Do you still have that lost kitten poster?"

"Probably," I said.

"Show it to Tony and Sam," he suggested. "They never saw it."

I dug into my bag and pulled it out. I passed it around.

"So what?" Sam commented, then added, "I've seen weirder."

A.G. took the poster and held it gingerly.

"After I left Nora, I had a good hamburger," he

said. "I wasn't enjoying it. This thing kept coming to mind. To be precise, the gargoyle superimposed on the face of one kitten. I had seen it before."

"Where?" I asked.

"In a newspaper photo."

"And?"

"It was a photo of a building in the Flatiron District—Twenty-first Street, if I remember correctly."

"Some kind of landmark preservation fight? Save the gargoyles," I offered.

"Oh, no! Not at all. It was a photo of the building in front of which Baby Kate and her sitter were last sighted."

I was dumbfounded.

Tony exploded: "Who the hell is Baby Kate?"

I didn't reprimand him. After all, Tony hasn't read a paper other than *Backstage* in twenty years.

A.G. said softly, "Baby Kate is, alive or dead, worth a cool million dollars, plus or minus ten percent."

Chapter 7

Thirty minutes later, we were all in A.G.'s apartment on 12th Street. We watched as he excavated carton after carton, looking for what he referred to as simply "the file." Obviously, poor dear A.G. kept files on many things. His obsessions led him to squirrel-like behavior.

It was Sam Tully who whispered to me: "You know, honey, squirrels only find thirty-eight percent of the acorns they bury. How does that grab you?"

The kittens, Billy and Bob, or whatever their names were, had joined happily in the search, climbing all over everything, peering into everything, rolling over everything.

I proceeded to tell Tony what I remembered about Baby Kate: "It happened about four or five years ago. The little girl, Kate, was four years old. She was abducted by her baby-sitter and a ransom was demanded. The baby-sitter was an actress named Paula Fite, with a funny stage name, something like Frankie Arkette. The parents didn't call the police at first. They paid a ransom. Neither the money nor the child was recovered."

"How much was the ransom?" Tony asked.

"Never disclosed."

"What was A.G. talking about? A million?"

"I figure he was talking about the reward," Sam said. "It must be close to a million by now. I remember the parents guaranteed five hundred grand. It was the biggest reward ever offered. And that was then. Hell, just the interest over five years on five hundred grand pushes it over the top."

"The parents must be filthy rich," Tony noted.

Much, much more was coming back to me. Like many New Yorkers, I had been momentarily absorbed by the case . . . much like the Etan Patz case of twenty years ago—a child abducted off a Soho Street and never seen again—still unsolved.

I said: "Well, yes. At least the wife was rich. Prosper. That was their name. Timothy and Hannah Prosper. He was one of those novelists who got good reviews and never sold more than 2,500 copies. She owned and ran an interior design company that specialized in putting plants and gardens in suburban corporate headquarters and office buildings. I think . . ."

My comments were interrupted by a whoop of joy. A.G. was doing a little dance, so inappropriate for a lawyer, holding up a newspaper clipping. He passed it around. No doubt about it. The clipping was from the *Daily News* a few days after the police learned of the kidnapping. It included a photo of the building on West 21st Street in front of which the baby-sitter and Baby Kate were last seen.

There were several gargoyles on the building, but only one of them was the exact duplicate of the one pasted over the kitten's face in the poster.

"Not only is it the same gargoyle," said Sam, "this same goddamn clipping was used for that poster."

He was right. Whoever had composed the poster had cut out the gargoyle from the newspaper article.

"So what?" Tony asked. "Maybe ten thousand people clipped that photo that day."

A.G. thrust his face forward, a bit aggressively, and said: "Ladies and gentlemen, I think it is time we broadened the inquiry."

"You mean a shot at a million dollars is too good to pass up?" Tony asked cynically.

"I mean," A.G. responded, "that we have a strong connection . . . a stable link . . . a pathway."

Tony cursed him. A.G. spat a curse back. My, my, my—Alice's ex-lovers were acting up.

I didn't know what to make of the gargoyle coincidence. It was a stretch. After all, I had no proof that the kitten poster had anything to do with the murders at all. Much less with Baby Kate.

I said to A.G.: "Why don't you serve some drinks."

He was quick to comply. It defused the situation. Tony had a beer. A.G. and Sam had bourbon on the rocks. I had a ginger ale.

The kittens discovered Sam and began to climb all over him. He beamed and started one of his lectures on the brilliance of his fictional detective, Harry Bondo.

I may have neglected to say before that Tully was working hard to resurrect his Harry Bondo mystery series by making Harry a gentler, kinder, and more logical detective.

The old Harry was a sort of caveman as well as a racist, woman-hating, homophobic sonofabitch.

"Harry," Sam went on, "would look at the gargoyles and apply a kind of feline reason. Can you dig it? I believe—"

"What the hell are you talking about?" Tony retorted, trying to crush the monologue before the old man got up a full head of steam.

Unfortunately, Sam was quite willing to discuss and explain Bondo's appropriation of feline logic.

"Very simple. My cat is sitting on the kitchen table looking out the window. Something flutters by outside and lands on the fire escape. My cat Pickles don't know what the hell it is. He can't figure out size or shape from such a distance. But so what? He goes for it! He goes for the flutter! Boom! He's gone! Out the window and onto the fire escape! Because to Pickles, his intuitive logic says—Move, Stupid. Bird."

What happened next, I am very proud of. I acted in a very Zen manner. Like a Zen swordsman or a Zen flower arranger. I wasn't really acting out of any bloody thing but intuition.

Boldly, I walked to the phone, picked up the cordless receiver, and dialed the Red Witch.

Cynthia answered. I asked her if an actress named either Paula Fite or Frankie Arkette had ever worked at the Red Witch.

She consulted the list she had given the police.

"Yes. There was a Frankie Arkette here. In 1992. For about five months."

I hung up the phone, rather elegantly, and announced the findings.

Then I added: "Yes, by all means, we broaden the inquiry."

A.G. was happy. Sam said nothing. He was no doubt thinking of Pickles's feline logic.

But Tony seemed to go around the bend. "Are you crazy, Swede?"

Ooooh. I didn't like it when he called me that. But I said nothing.

He kept on: "Half the out-of-work actresses in New York over the past twenty years have worked tables at the Red Witch!"

It was too late. It didn't matter what he said. I was caught up, enthralled. I had pounced through that window, onto the fire escape.

Chapter 8

A.G. gave me the Prosper home address, from his files, I assume. It was a beautiful little red-brick building just off Irving Place, a block and a half from Gramercy Park.

Hannah Prosper Enterprises was housed further downtown, in a warehouse with an attached indoor garden shed close by the Fulton Fish Market.

If Timothy was still a working novelist, I reasoned, then it was he who would be at home, and I prepped myself for the encounter by purchasing a paperback of the only novel of his that seemed to be still in print. At least that's what the saleswoman at the Barnes & Noble on Union Square said to me when *Ice of Hearts* was located.

I strode to the intercom on that freezing morning around ten-thirty and rang the bell with a flourish.

But I had no plan other than simply to make contact with the one who was there; to probe, to confront, to inquire. Let's face it. I was embarked on a precarious journey inspired by one lousy gargoyle floating about, and two very old dead friends, and perhaps a million dollars.

There was no question about my distress. I mean, I was a prime suspect in a homicide involving two people I had loved and whose deaths were directly related to a whim of mine.

No wonder I leaned on the bell.

"Who's there?"

What a mundane question.

"Hello. I'm Alice Nestleton. Are you Timothy Prosper?"

"What do you want?"

"I have to talk to you."

"About what?"

Lie, Alice. Lie, lie, lie. Get in there. The best lie— that I had information that might help find his child—I could not bring myself to enunciate. No, I could not do that.

But the lie I did think of was so ridiculous—"I want to talk to you about *Ice of Hearts*"—that he just vanished from the other end of the line and refused to answer when I rang again.

I walked to a coffee shop on 17th Street just east of Irving Place. A tiny café with five tables and chairs. I ordered a cappuccino and a strange-looking breadstick, and asked for butter and jelly on the side. No jelly, they informed me. Now, that was depressing.

I sat, sipped, chewed, and thought. Then I opened Mr. Prosper's novel, *Ice of Hearts*, and began to read.

Was I looking for a mushroom and sour cream recipe? Hardly.

He was a good writer. But it was an old-fashioned novel. Sort of in the Kay Boyle mold. I read about twenty pages. The plot was apparent. A rather naive American professor ends up in Venice and falls in love with a very nasty beautiful woman with dangerous friends.

I then turned to the back cover and looked at the bottom of the page where there was a small photo of the author along with a brief biography.

He had a plain-looking, thin face with light, receding hair. The expression on his face made it appear as if his eyes hurt him. The photo was a head-and-shoulders shot. But I could make out that he was wearing a wool sleeveless sweater.

The bio said he was born in San Francisco in 1955; this was his third novel; he had taught at the University of Virginia and NYU; he had had several plays mounted by the New Playwrights Collective; and he now lived in Manhattan with his family.

That was it. That was enough! I was startled, to say the least.

I too had been part of the New Playwrights Collective. It was a group that workshopped new plays in a storefront theater in downtown Brooklyn, close by the old Navy Yard. The project ran out of funds after eighteen months. No one was paid. No one cared. It was good fun while it lasted. I must have acted in about twenty plays for them—all kinds of roles. When had that been? Probably '85 or '86.

What a bizarre conjunction! I stared at the photo. I just didn't remember the face. Maybe if they had listed his plays I would have remembered him. I sat back and kept staring at that face. I remembered Cynthia's *cri de coeur* that these murders weren't about the Red Witch Restaurant; they weren't about menus. They were about grudges, she said. Some crazy actor or director was behind the killings.

It looked as if she was right about the mushrooms and sour cream. And maybe by extension, Baby Kate. I realized it might be time for me to speak to the NYPD again. I had an obligation to reveal the gargoyle conjunction to them.

Yes, it might well jeopardize our chance to reap a very substantial reward. But I wasn't in this mess for the money, was I? After all, I am, was, and always will be a pillar of the community.

But I didn't make the call right away. I sat there with my half-eaten breadstick and my now cold cappuccino, and stared at Prosper's book. The cover design was pretty compelling—a silhouette of an erotically entwined couple with icicles hanging off their naked feet like grotesque toenails.

The thought came to me that I should write a novel someday. But what about? I smiled grimly. It would have to be about that kiss I witnessed between the aging lovers Alex and Lila, before my stupid idea of recreating their nuptial meal sent them into what my grandmother used to call wistfully "the other side." Then I started to rummage for a quarter.

Isn't it odd that the deaths of Alex and Lila occurred because I had enough money to fund a stupid whim, money that came from a lucrative bit part in a TV cop show pilot?

And here I was again, back in another TV cop show. At least it seemed that way.

I met with Detectives Greco and Fontana at a donut shop on West 14th Street. I had told them why I wanted to meet with them—to reveal a few interesting facts I'd discovered. But when they showed up, they became a bit aggressive—as if they were in the TV show "Law and Order," as if I were a suspect who had really called them to cut a deal. How I loathed those cop shows!

When it became apparent that they had the wrong script, they just glowered and stared out of the window at their double-parked unmarked car, which was causing chaos to the traffic pattern on 14th

Street. They wouldn't even buy a donut, although Fontana did have black coffee. It also seemed to irritate them that I was nibbling at a chocolate glaze.

When all the preliminaries were out of the way, I placed on the counter, with a flourish, the two revealing items: the kitten poster and the building photo.

On the latter I had circled the gargoyle that corresponded to the one superimposed over the third kitten's face.

Then, without further ado, I laid out my theories. One, that the kitten poster had something to do with the deaths of Alex and Lila.

Two, that (a) the gargoyle pictured in both items and (b) the fact that Baby Kate's sitter had once worked at the Red Witch, and (c) the fact that Timothy Prosper, the father of Baby Kate, was a playwright with experience in the New York theater world all seemed to point to a strong connection between the sour cream murders and the unsolved kidnapping.

Then I threw in for good measure what Sam Tully had heard about the murdered waiter, and reported his speculation that the killing of Jerrard was about an unpaid loan and nothing more.

It was a mouthful. I ate some more of my donut and waited.

Greco said quickly: "We know about the loan shark. It may or may not be meaningful."

The two detectives passed the gargoyles back and forth between them.

When they began to turn the pieces upside down and stare at them, it dawned on me that maybe they weren't so impressed with my deductions.

"This is great stuff," Greco said.

"Right on the money!" said Fontana.

"We're going to use this," said Greco.

"It makes sense out of a lot of stuff we just couldn't figure before," said Fontana.

Greco held the kitten poster up in the air and explained: "And if you look at it a certain way, it takes you right inside that Fifty-seventh Street walk-up with that dish being delivered. It takes you right smack into that sour cream and mushroom dish. It takes you right there—the guests, the host, the delivery boy. Lady, you are one hell of an investigator."

Fontana leaned over and whispered in my ear: "I hear you're also working on the Lindbergh kidnapping. You keep me informed. The whole department is waiting on this."

And they walked out. A little humiliation is a healthy thing. I looked at my watch. It was only two o'clock in the afternoon. Let them mock me all they wanted, I was on the case.

It wasn't easy to locate the offices of Hannah Prosper. Her firm was on a street just north of the Fulton Fish Market. And there was no sign at all on the warehouse-type building.

Once inside, I requested to meet with Hannah

Prosper on a personal matter. I was grilled without mercy by a trim, middle-aged woman in a black Flax dress. She was, she claimed, Hannah's executive assistant. Her name was Millie.

"Are you sure you're not here concerning the missing child?"

"Quite sure," I lied.

"Mrs. Prosper has no use for psychics and that sort. Do you understand me?"

"I fully understand."

Millie did not trust me at all. She did not think I understood what she was telling me, so she spelled it out.

"Look, Mrs. Prosper is no longer a well woman. What happened to her family left terrible scars. She shouldn't even be working anymore. Now, I will let you see her if and only if those personal matters you speak of do not have anything at all to do with the kidnapping."

"I was in a theater group with her husband about ten years ago. All I want is to see if she remembers a few people we all knew in common, and where I could find them now."

She looked at me hard, as if trying to gauge my honesty. Then she walked through a door and came back in three minutes.

"Go ahead," she said, and raised a cautionary finger.

I entered Hannah's office. It was really just a space

filled with long aluminum drafting desks. On the walls were maintenance records for her various plant installations in Manhattan office buildings.

The space opened out into a large, low, glass-covered greenhouse groaning with plants of all kinds and small trees in tubs. Scattered throughout the greenhouse were many "dollhouses" constructed of clear plastic and festooned with thermometers and hoses, obviously for special plants with particular growing needs. It was hard to believe that this was downtown Manhattan and not an enchanted rain forest.

Hannah Prosper was seated on a small swivel stool, staring at the maintenance records on the wall. She was wearing a gardener's worksuit and a bandanna.

I approached. She looked up. Her face had obviously once been pretty; now it was a puffy, painful blank.

I had never in my life seen a person who looked so abysmally unhappy. Yet whatever medication she was taking, and it must have been a great deal, seemed to have given her a series of scripts so that she could proceed with her life.

"Millie told me your name," she said, then gestured with her hand that she had forgotten the name. I noticed that the brown hair visible under the front of the bandanna was very thin in front, as if from radiation treatment or malnutrition or the side effects of medication.

"Alice Nestleton."

"And you know Tim?"

"We were in the New Playwrights Collective."

"Yes. A long time ago, wasn't it? But I was never a theater person. I like tennis and hiking. I like . . ." She suddenly stopped talking, as if she were watching her words leave her mouth and she loathed them.

I cursed myself for bothering this crushed mother. But when would I get such an opportunity again? I searched for a method. I searched for something to dangle in front of her that would be detached from the loss of her child, but would shine some light on everything. Why I had not anticipated her distress, I don't know. Why I hadn't formulated scenarios and questions before I arrived there, I don't know.

Fasten on the party in the 57th Street apartment, I intuited. Focus on the guests at that party. That was my hook.

"Do you know a musician named Lister?"

"No. But you must ask my husband. He will remember everybody in that theater group."

"Your husband will not speak to me."

She nodded, as if this was not unusual.

"What about a photographer named Brad Carmody?"

"No."

"A comic who doubles as a waiter—named Jim Jerrard?"

"No."

"A baker named Nozak?"

"No."

"He supplies restaurants. He's a very good baker."

"No."

"Are you sure you don't know him? He supplied the Red Witch. You know, Alex and Lila's restaurant. Do you know them? Alex Woodward. Lila Huggins. Old people."

"Why do you keep asking me about people I don't know? Who are you? What do you want?"

She suddenly stood up and started to scream. "Millie, Millie!"

The black Flax lady rushed in. Hannah Prosper seemed to go into a trance. Millie took me firmly by the arm and led me out.

"Believe me," I said, "I did not mention the kidnapping."

"She's okay maybe one day out of ten, and this is not that day."

I left, profoundly uncomfortable.

Chapter 9

I made my pronouncement to the faithful assembled in my loft.

"Forget the wife. She's a pathetic cripple. If there is a link between the murders and the kidnapping, Timothy Prosper is the one who knows it or forged it. That is my considered judgment."

It was a well-attended meeting, a day after my contact with the Prospers. Even Nora had showed up.

And everyone seemed to be listening to what I said with great interest.

Except Basillio.

He was seated on a window ledge, staring down onto the street below. He was thinking, his head moving a bit from side to side, as if he was silently debating and discarding alternatives.

I felt a sudden sense of desolation.

I knew Tony Basillio so well. I knew his cryptic behavior patterns. This one meant he had met one of those fetching young actresses; that he was about to get involved with her. Where did they meet? Probably at a party. That's where he usually met them. He could not resist those fey creatures, and they could not resist him.

Poor Tony. The desolation vanished. We were not lovers anymore. I felt sorry for him. The man was getting older fast, while his tastes were running to younger and younger female company. A recipe for disaster.

When I was young and promiscuous at the Guthrie Theatre in Minneapolis, at least I always fell head over heels in love with a guy before I slept with him. And it never had anything to do with what he looked like. It always had to do with his eccentricities, his panache—how he banged a plate down or how he described an acting teacher.

Suddenly Tony looked up; he was glaring at me. He always blamed me for his philandering. Me. What a lovable fool.

"A.G. took the floor next, waving a sheaf of papers and announcing. "What I've got to say has more to do with the mercenary side of this investigation."

He stood at the head of my long, narrow, beat-up dining room table as if he were addressing the jury. Again he waved that bundle of papers.

"I spoke a bit prematurely the other day. After

some careful inquiries and calculations, I have come to the conclusion that a downward revision is in order."

"What the hell are you talking about?" Tully demanded.

"The reward, my friend, the reward," A.G. replied. "It's not a million. The total is currently about $667,000. That would be a split of $133,400 each."

There was silence.

A.G. continued: "Perhaps it would be best if we incorporated."

Again, there was a long silence, punctuated only by some high-pitched complaints by Pancho, who was unhappy that Sam had picked him up and was staring at him nose to nose.

I forgot to mention that Sam believed in a bizarre theory of reincarnation. It was his theory that Pancho probably was his great aunt, because of his stumpy half tail. His theory about cats who live in bars—and there seem to be thousands of such felines in Manhattan—is too bizarre even to recount.

Nora broke the human silence.

"May I say something?" she asked deferentially.

"By all means," I replied encouragingly.

What followed was in no way deferential. She began to shout.

"Are you all mad? *Incorporating*? For what? Everyone knows Baby Kate is dead. And if ten thousand cops and FBI agents couldn't find the child or her body—or the kidnapper—or the ransom money—do you honestly think we can? Do you really think so? How did we get this far into lunacy? We were just supposed to help Alice find out who murdered her friends. But no! Instead, you dig up one or two peculiar facts about an old crime, then tie it to Alice's problem by some very imaginative logic. And we're suddenly playing Pinkerton Agents and Sam Spade. Yes, by all means . . . incorporate. And let's get posh offices and beautiful stationery. What about pistol permits? Hey, yeah, and Burberry raincoats for those stormy nights of surveillance. My God, can you see how crazy we're all becoming?"

It was some speech.

Tony, suddenly alert and happy that Nora was upset, suggested a referendum with secret balloting. There was a collective groan of protest, but Tony would not be dissuaded.

The vote, he said, should deal with three questions on a straight up or down vote:

Proposition One: Should the Baby Kate investigation be continued?

Proposition Two: Should we incorporate?

Proposition Three: Do we have enough evidence to conclude that the Baby Kate kidnapping is somehow linked to the Alex and Lila murders?

I cut up some plain white paper into strips and distributed the slips. We voted, Tony grinning evilly at Nora as he filled in his ballots. Sam Tully collected the slips, unfolded them, and tallied the results.

The results were:

On Proposition One: 3 yeas; 2 nays

On Proposition Two: 2 yeas; 3 nays

On Proposition Three: 1 yea; 1 nay; 3 abstentions

Seizing upon the referendum results, I quickly distributed assignments.

Tony was to shadow Timothy Prosper.

A.G. was to read Mr. Prosper's novels and other works.

Nora was to use her contacts to dig up the hidden life of Alex and Lila, if such a thing existed. And to find any and all threads connecting them to Paula Fite a.k.a. Frankie Arkette . . . to any and all persons associated with the defunct New Playwrights Collective . . . to anyone strange or interesting in a criminal sense.

Sam and I would track down Prosper's friends and academic colleagues and nose around at his last known place of work—New York University.

After the assignments were distributed, I served Afrika cookies, the thin chocolate wafers I'm crazy about, with 2 percent milk.

The other options were tea and coffee. No takers on those. But Sam wanted hot chocolate. "It being winter and all," he pointed out.

I could not accommodate him.

The troops began to trickle out. Soon only Nora was left. She still looked upset. I cleaned up around her.

"Tell me," she said, "do the police still consider you a suspect?"

"Yes."

"Well, to be honest, Alice, I would too—in their place."

Then she broke into ironic laughter. "I could have prevented it, you know. I mean, when you showed up with that ridiculous dinner idea, all I had to say was 'Sorry, no, too busy.' And believe me, those dishes were so stupid that I did want to refuse. I thought you were drunk. But I couldn't turn you down. You're my friend. My best friend."

"You don't have to tell me how dumb my idea was, Nora. But it's all hindsight now. At the time I thought it one of the sweetest gifts I ever gave anyone."

"Sweet? No. Never. Never sweet. Stupid. Besides, you told me they were English. But mushrooms fried in butter and topped with sour cream is a Russian dish. Pure Russian."

There was no reasoning with her now. Like the abortion issue, both sides were right.

What dreams I had that night! Terrible, crazy ones—and they were all about food. Specifically, about sour cream and mushrooms.

I had to go onstage and recite dozens of recipes, all of which called for sour cream and/or mushrooms. But when I tried to speak, my mind went blank. I could not remember a single recipe.

My ex-husband even turned up in one of the

dreams. In it, I was transported to where he now lived: among the Eskimos of Hudson Bay.

He was waiting for me in his igloo, along with his new wife, who was bare-breasted. The two of them were dipping chunks of raw seal into a can and then popping the shiny, dripping things into their mouths. He didn't know the recipes either. In fact, he didn't say a word. But he did pick up a harpoon and hurl it through the wall of the snow house. When I heard some creature scream, I woke up, freezing and afraid and alone in the loft.

That was one dream I couldn't even begin to decipher. Nor did I want to.

I put on four sweaters, took two aspirin, drank a huge cup of camomile tea with lemon, and fell asleep again.

As I left the house that morning to meet Sam at his Spring Street apartment, I had the sudden realization that the Inuit wife in the dream—that bare-breasted, blubber-chewing woman—had Nora's face. That in itself was disturbing enough. But then, I thought, no, no, maybe it wasn't Nora's face. Maybe it was the face of the gargoyle from the lost kittens poster.

Sam was already downstairs, waiting. Even though it was a cold morning and there were wisps of snow swirling about, he was wearing nothing but his moth-eaten sweatshirt and stained trousers, with a muffler tied to the point of strangulation around his neck. He looked like an old bear who had lost his way in the woods.

I was wearing earmuffs and my trusty Goodwill winter coat, a three-quarter length, green fake-leather thing with sheepskin lining. I guess I looked like an out-of-work bear trainer.

We worked out our strategy over breakfast in a croissant shop on Broadway where they make a great corn muffin.

"Let me do the talking," I told Sam.

He stared into his coffee. "Doll, I wouldn't have it any other way."

Then we walked to the large New York University Information Center near the east side of Washington Square Park.

It was filled with students, with stacks of catalogs, and with what seemed to be hundreds of announcements of clubs, services, and events plastered on the walls.

A young Indian or Pakistani man with a small white-and-blue flower in his lapel was eager to help.

I told him our prefabricated story. We were academic book publishers from San Francisco.

We were supposed to pick up a manuscript from an NYU professor named Timothy Prosper. But our signals got crossed and he had already left for Europe by the time we arrived.

So he must have left the manuscript in his office, or with a colleague, for us to pick up.

The clerk punched "Prosper" into his desktop computer, then fiddled a bit with the keyboard. Finally he announced, "Professor Prosper is no longer on the NYU faculty."

Dr. Prosper no longer at the university? Oh, dear. Something awful must have happened. We had to straighten this mess out. The publisher was waiting for Dr. Prosper's manuscript. Did he have any suggestions for where we might turn next?

The guard gave us the address of a building on West 3rd Street that housed the Writers in Residence Program, which Prosper had been part of.

Sam and I marched over. It was an old building.

"Do you realize, Sam, that we are only a block or so away from the Red Witch?"

He nodded and pointed upward. There were gargoyles on the cornices of the building. But not our grisly little charmers. Were they friendly? I waved at one of them.

The WIR program was on the eighth floor.

We stepped from the elevator into a tiny ancient anteroom with a metal desk behind which sat an informally dressed young woman, a student most likely working off her tuition.

I presented our cover story once again.

The young lady listened attentively and patiently, although she never stopped working at her current task—stuffing envelopes with some kind of crested invitations.

I finished my tale, but before she could reply, two bellows interrupted her.

"Whoa! Whoa!"

The noise had come from just inside one of the narrow halls that radiated out from the anteroom.

The moon-faced man who had shouted at us was short and very fat, so fat he filled the hallway completely.

He was wearing jeans with suspenders, a bright, bright red flannel shirt, and one of the ugliest floppy green ties I have ever seen. It was swinging back and forth across his huge stomach like a windshield wiper.

He was three-quarters bald but with huge tufts of hair spiraling out of the sides of his head, just above his ears. His large nose was crisscrossed with prominent veins. Three guesses who attended the faculty's annual Halloween party as W. C. Fields without spending a dime on a costume.

Since I have always had—for unknown reasons— a great affection for fat people, I was instantly charmed, although it was obvious he was in an aggressive mood. After all, the term "whoa" is usually used for horses.

Then he lumbered, or rolled, into the room and moved quite close to us . . . looking us over critically, clinically, as if we were on the auction block.

It was then that I noticed his outfit was completed

by sandals—no socks—a rather daring eccentricity in the dead of winter.

I looked down at his pudgy, dead-white toes as he circled us.

Having completed the inspection, he moved his bulk backward and announced: "I am Porter Boudreau, acting director of the Writers in Residency Program, and I can say without fear of contradiction that your story is the most egregious bullshit I have ever heard."

He paused. He smiled.

To Sam, he said: "You are too old to be a cop."

To me, he said: "And you're too tall."

"For a policewoman, you mean?" I said.

"For anything," he answered. To the student secretary, he said: "Miss Sansom, what say you? If they are not police officers, what in heaven's name are they? And why would they show up claiming they are searching for a manuscript that does not exist? And how do I know that no such work exists? Because to my certain knowledge poor Timothy has not written a word since Kate was lifted.

"Are they foreign spies then, Miss Sansom? Dispatched by Japanese publishers in desperate search of a best-seller? Sadly, no. Even when Timothy was writing and publishing, his novels were lamentable commercial failures. Not for lack of excellence, mind you, but unregenerate failures nonetheless.

"So, Miss Sansom, if they are not the law and not literary pirates, they must be bill collectors. Yes? No! Dear Hannah Prosper is loaded, and always bails her husband out of his financial difficulties.

"What then are we left with? Who could they be?" He chuckled diabolically. "Journalists, that's what. Execrable journalists. Resurrecting that hideous kidnapping with some kind of new angle. Feeding off the misery of a poor bereft husband and wife for the delectation of their ghoulish readers.

"The only question remaining, Miss Sansom: What do we do with them? Shall we call Security? No, not a bit of it. I suggest we fling them from the window. It's high enough that they'll crunch and splatter when they hit."

"You try it, Fatso," Tully threatened, "and I'll let the air out of your tire."

I slid between them.

"All right, Professor Boudreau. You're right. I concocted a story in order to meet Timothy Prosper's colleagues. It seems to have worked."

He laughed at the confessional arrogance of my statement.

"Madam, wouldn't it have been easier to simply call Timothy and ask him the names of his colleagues?"

"He won't speak to me."

"I wonder why."

"Perhaps because I want to help him. Some people cannot abide help."

My explanation seemed to satisfy Professor Boudreau. No doubt he knew that any couple who had suffered such a wrenching experience as the kidnapping of a child could use any kind of help from any source, even if they resisted. He inclined his head in a kind of bow to both of us—an apology.

Then he said: "So, here is where we stand. You are neither cops nor bill collectors nor literary pirates nor reporters. You simply want to help Timothy Prosper in a matter on which he wants no help. And you are looking for friends of Prosper to help you achieve your selfless goal. Well, look no further. I was his colleague. And his drinking companion. I remain his friend. I am even the defender of his literary reputation. But, alas, the man is avoiding me at present."

He pointed down the hallway. "Please enter the first cave on the right. I shall bring coffee after I have emptied my errant bladder. Which, as I have become older, is now like a playful dolphin in a murky sea."

The office was small, of course, but generously high ceilinged. He returned with mugs of coffee and macaroons on a wicker platter and eased himself down behind the desk. He distributed the repast, then said:

"So, I have ascertained that your motives are pure. You are offering help of some kind to the Prospers, and no two people on earth need help as much as they. But, to be honest, as I said, my friendship with

Tim is in abeyance. He is no longer in residence here. He no longer seeks or welcomes my company."

He suddenly sat straight up, pointed a fat finger at Sam, and said: "I know you."

"I don't think so," Sam replied, distinctly unfriendly.

"*Yes, yes, yes,* I know you," Boudreau insisted, then closed his eyes and buried his expansive face in his hands, trying to retrieve the memory.

Then he opened one eye. His face flushed; those reddish veins across his nose throbbed. He smashed his hand down on the desk like a hammer and exclaimed: "You are the creator of the most ridiculous private eye in the history of fiction. You are the imagination—more or less—behind Harry Bondo."

"Ridiculous, you sonofabitch!"

"Now, now. Please do not take offense. I meant not so much 'ridiculous' as 'quixotic.' I've always wanted to meet the man who wrote *Only the Dead Wear Socks*—and whose photo graces the back cover."

Sam calmed down and lit a cigarette. I realized none of this would have transpired if we had simply called on the professor and introduced ourselves like sane, normal people. He already knew who Sam Tully was—so now I gave him the name Alice Nestleton. It did not ring any kinds of bells for him.

"Do you write mysteries too?" I asked.

"No."

"Regular novels?"

"No. I am a literary historian. I am famous, or notorious, for an obscure article in a journal which ballooned into a wonderful controversy in 1981. In that article I proved that one of the greatest short poems in our language—"Leda and the Swan," by William Butler Yeats—was written to honor Mussolini and Italian fascism. And, in a sense, it has been downhill ever since for me. Ah, yes, Porter Boudreau, the downhill racer of academe . . . that's me. Tim and I used to discuss that all the time—who was moving downhill faster."

"Did you say you often ate together?"

"No. Never. We didn't believe in eating during the day. What we did together was drink. Three times a week usually."

"At one of the nearby places, like the bars on Waverly?" I pressed.

"Oh, no! We would go uptown to the Museum Pub, on East 81st Street."

"Why the hell would you go all the way up there?" Sam asked.

"I haven't the slightest idea. The man, though I love him dearly, is a bit strange. But he was paying. His money, his choice. Isn't that the proper etiquette? I am a fat man with thin corners."

He burst out laughing at his own metaphor; I couldn't join in the appreciative laughter because, frankly, it made no sense to me.

"Did you ever go to a café called the Red Witch with him? It's only a few blocks from here."

"Never heard of it. What a silly name for a restaurant. I don't like that name at all. It's childish, wouldn't you say?"

Sam asked impatiently: "Did the man ever talk about gargoyles?"

"About what?"

"You heard me. Gargoyles. You know, those . . . those little monster things . . . on buildings. Did he ever say he liked them?"

"Well, he liked me," Professor Boudreau quipped. "But no, I don't recall him mentioning such objects. I think I would have remembered if he exhibited any interest in those morbid things. I mean, I was always telling him that his novels lacked the requisite morbidity to sell well."

He paused, stared at the ceiling as if something or someone was walking around on it, and then added, "I myself have always had a wonderful visual memory of the Classic Comic of *The Hunchback of Notre Dame*. The cover featured the hideously deformed Quasimodo high up on the massive church, clutching a gargoyle even more hideous than himself. Yes, no doubt, it is I, not Tim, who might be a gargoyleophile."

"Did Prosper run a tab at the Museum Pub?" Sam asked.

"Oh, yes. Till all the seas gang dry. Bless him."

Then Porter Boudreau kicked off one sandal and

launched into a monologue on Timothy Prosper's novel—*Ice of Hearts*—which was so abstruse and goofy that, when it was over, all I could do was thank him for his efforts and then wander out of the building in a dazed state—and call off all further efforts for the day.

I took a cab home, dumping Sam at a bar on Varick Street along the way, and fell asleep fully clothed twenty seconds after I entered my loft. Bush and Pancho, gentlemen that they were, left me utterly alone.

The phone woke me at 2 P.M. It was Sam.

"You up?"

"And alert," I lied.

"We got some work to do, honey. You know that?"

"You mean that pub, don't you?"

"Damn right. Why is that guy up there all the time? He lives and works downtown. Why go up to Eighty-first and Madison and run a tab? It don't make sense, honey. Yeah, you gotta pay that pub a visit. But listen, you better take A.G. along instead of me. It's a white bread kind of place. They don't trust people who don't have good teeth. Get me?"

"Okay. I'll call A.G."

"What did you think of Chubby?"

"I liked him."

"Yeah, I did too. In a way. Did you pick up that he ain't straight?"

"Yes."

"Yeah, you just know it. It's not any one thing. It's just there, like a pineapple on a kitchen table."

I hesitated a bit before I asked. "Do you think Prosper is bisexual?"

"You mean him and Chubby? No way. You're missing what's going on there. Believe me, I've seen it before."

"What is going on?"

"Well, that guy is no spring chicken; I mean Boudreau. He's got that old gay sensibility. When gays were in the closet, being gay was about fraternity. Gays would fret over, take care of, hang around with strange straights. Straights in trouble. Get me?"

"Not really, Sam. Besides, in what way is Prosper strange?"

"Don't know yet, honey. But he sure as hell is."

He hung up. I made a cup of coffee and called A.G. Roth. The man sounded depressed.

"I need your help tomorrow, A.G."

"That's what I'm here for."

"We have to go to a bar uptown."

"Sure."

"You sound terrible."

"I don't like the kittens. They're harassing me. And I don't like Timothy Prosper's novels."

"All this will pass, A.G."

"You mean like our time has passed, Alice? Like

our love flared once and then crawled back into oblivion?''

My, my, he was in bad shape. Numbskull metaphors and all. But I was in no mood to dispense therapy to the lovelorn. I rang off.

The phone rang again in two minutes. Had he composed a sonnet in the interim? I suddenly felt very guilty. I was not behaving well.

I picked up the receiver and greeted him tenderly.

It wasn't A.G.

It was a woman who identified herself as Luann Campion, an NYPD detective still working the Baby Kate case. She wanted to see me as soon as possible. Well now, wasn't that interesting, I thought. Detectives Fontana and Greco had obviously thought twice about the gargoyles.

Detective Campion arrived at about 4 P.M. She came alone. I made her a cup of orange pekoe tea. She was a short, slim, Hispanic woman, maybe Cuban, definitely not Peruvian, and she wore a running suit, running shoes, and a turned-around baseball cap. She was absolutely the youngest looking police detective I had ever seen.

She spoke simply, in a low voice tinged with a New York accent.

''Two homicide detectives told me you have something on Baby Kate . . . I'll take what I can get.''

I laid the gargoyles out on the dining room table.

She studied the two pieces of paper without touching them.

"And you also think, Miss Nestleton, that my case and their case connect. Right?"

"Right."

"Why? I mean, why, other than the gargoyle cha-cha-cha?"

"First of all, because Paula Fite worked at the Red Witch."

"A long time ago."

"Right, a long time ago, and briefly. Second, Timothy Prosper used to be in the theater."

Detective Luann Campion smiled at me after I spoke those words. It was a smile of both derision and compassion for me. She was telling me there were three million souls in, on, and about the theater in New York, and one third of them seem to have worked at the Red Witch at one time or another.

Then she turned back to the gargoyles. She stared at them. "You know, we get sightings of Baby Kate and her sitter from all over the country. Oh, yes, last week someone spotted them in Vancouver. The week before, in Atlanta. And believe it or not, five or six in Newark, New Jersey, over the years. Sightings, that is. So actually it's kind of pleasant, following up a lead in downtown Manhattan."

She laughed. Then she tapped the papers. Tap, tap, tap. Then she said: "Tell me all about these little fellows."

As I recounted for her essentially what I had recounted to the two homicide detectives, she kept picking the poster up and turning it around and around in her hands, as if determining the technical aspects of the item—what kind of paper it was, how the poster had been prepared, how it was printed, how it was Xeroxed. She had to do this, for it was obvious that Lila had received a Xerox of the original poster.

She asked me: "Is there any doubt in your mind that the photos in the poster are your friend's kittens?"

"Some doubt. I don't really know. It could be them. But maybe not. Kittens tend to resemble each other."

"And this phone number on the poster?"

"It turned out to be a pay phone in Lincoln Center."

At that specific point in our conversation, her demeanor toward me changed. She began to take me and my information seriously. I interpreted that change as stemming from the Lincoln Center location of the pay phone. It must have touched a nerve.

"Was a Lincoln Center pay phone involved in the Baby Kate kidnapping?" I asked.

She smiled but didn't answer. Then she said: "You seem to be hellbent on making a connection between the two cases. Do you really think such a connection will take the heat off you?"

"No."

"Let's get back to Timothy Prosper. You say you were in a theater group with him in the 1980s."

"Correct."

"And that, in your mind, makes him a theater person."

"Yes."

"But you have no evidence that he knew this Alex—or Lila—or studied with them, or appeared with them."

"Correct."

"And you have no evidence that Hannah Prosper was ever likewise engaged."

"Correct."

"And what about Paula Fite? Also known as Frankie Arkette."

"As I said, all I know is that she worked briefly at the Red Witch."

"Well, let me tell you: We tracked down every conceivable lead in every place she ever performed. Other than her waitress stint in that restaurant, the names of your dead friends never came up."

"How much money was the ransom payment?" I asked.

"I can't tell you that."

"Who took that building photo?" I asked.

"A staff photographer at the *News*."

"How did he know it was the last place the sitter and the child were seen?"

"There's a parking lot across the street. The attendant saw them. He used to see them often, walking by on his side of the street—good-looking lady with a stroller. He wondered why they were on the other side of the street that day."

Detective Campion looked at Bushy, who was now sidling up to her tentatively.

"How often do you brush him?" she asked.

"Twice a week, if I remember," I replied. And then I wondered where she kept her weapon. I saw no bulge or holster of any kind.

She flicked out a small card from some mysterious recess and handed it to me.

"If you come on anything else, call me. By the way, I assume you are aware that a very large reward is in place."

"I am aware of that."

She smiled, but in a kindly manner, and then asked: "Is there anything else I should know?"

I didn't say a word.

She walked out. It is odd, I thought, that she made no mention of the mushroom and sour cream dish, not even a quip. Had I asked her the wrong questions? Had she asked me the wrong ones also?

Chapter 10

We met in the main ground floor gift shop of the Metropolitan Museum of Art. The Museum Pub was only two blocks away.

I was studying a copy of a book called *Women of Dada* when I saw A.G. enter. He didn't see me at first. There was a look of high expectation on his face. As if he were a young man again, meeting a girl in a museum. You know that look . . . who hasn't seen it in museums . . . the anticipation of young lovers as they meander from painting to painting. Their thoughts are a long way from oil and canvas, but they make such a good try at being students of art history.

Yet it was me A.G. was meeting. That look unnerved me. And made me sad. The longer I live, the less I really know about men. They are peculiar in many ways, but above all in their often inappropriate fevered anticipations. They never realize that.

When he saw me, the look vanished.

I took him by the hand and led him out of the gift shop to one of the circular benches in the lobby. I told him what we had to do.

We left the Met and entered the Museum Pub, on Madison and 81st Street, at thirty minutes past noon.

No wonder Sam had refused to accompany me; it was simply too charming for his sensibility. It was rather dark and woody inside. The small bar was empty. The restaurant area, however, was packed; dozens of people seated at small tables with bright checked cloths and a single small flower vase in the center of each table. The clientele looked like prosperous denizens of the area taking their maiden aunts to lunch. The menu outside the pub claimed they were famous for their honey-dipped chicken.

The plan was for A.G. to show the bartender the book photo of Prosper, claim he was an old friend who knew the writer drank here, inquire if the bartender knew him well, and then just let the conversation go where it might.

A.G. began brilliantly, ordering a brandy and coffee for himself and a Lillet on the rocks for me.

When the bartender, who was a big, redheaded young man, returned with the drinks, A.G. flashed the photo and started to talk.

The bud was nipped quickly.

The bartender raised his hands in protest.

"I don't know your friend," he said. "I don't know anyone here. I started three days ago, after they fired the regular guy. He had been here for about fifteen years."

"Do you know where we can find him?" I asked.

"I hear he hangs out at Rose's Tavern. That's on Lexington and Eighty-fifth."

"What's his name?"

"Dennis."

"Can you describe him?" A.G. asked.

A flash of suspicion on the young man's face. "What's this about?" he asked.

"I told you," A.G. said, a bit sternly, tapping the photo of Timothy Prosper.

The young man thought for a while. One could read his thoughts. They were not subtle. *Who are these people?* Who was he protecting? Then he grimaced and said, "Tall, skinny, bald, a bad eye. But I only saw him a few times." And then he signaled with his body language that if he knew anything else about this Dennis, he was keeping it to himself. We paid up and walked out without touching the drinks.

We headed toward Lexington Avenue, thoroughly frustrated.

The moment I saw the outside of Rose's Tavern, I realized that this place was what people used to call a joint, and I needed Sam with me rather than A.G. But there was no time for substitutions.

I remembered what Sam had once told me—
"Honey," he said, "do not try to sweet-talk or brow-beat a bartender. If you need information, pay for it. Up front and honest."

"A.G., do you have any cash on you?"

"Some."

"How much?"

"About $150."

"What kind of denominations?"

"Who cares?"

"I care!"

He opened his wallet. He had one fifty-dollar bill and the rest were twenties and tens.

"Let me have the fifty."

"What for?"

"In case we need it inside."

He gave me the bill. Then he said, "Look, we really need a new game plan now. This Dennis is not going to want to chat with us. He's just a customer in this place. He doesn't have to humor us."

"Let's just find him first. He may not even be in there."

"What I'm trying to say, Alice, is simply—what are we looking for?"

"I don't know. I don't really know. But for starters, A.G., how about why Timothy Prosper was drinking uptown all the time when he worked and lived downtown. It's surely not because there aren't any bars in the Village—or in his own neighborhood. Sam found that very peculiar. And Sam should know. So do I, find it peculiar."

We walked inside. It was grim. Smoky. Ugly. A dull noise permeating. Mostly middle-aged men along the bar, some older. Many TV sets on, but no sounds emanating from them. A jukebox playing Tony Bennett. The strange thud of beer bottles on counters. Some ice cubes in some glasses tinkling. The squeaking of barstools as they turned.

Shafts of blue and green light seemed to filter through the place from some unknown source. And there was a strong smell of wet winter clothes—wool.

A.G. and I walked along the line. Three-quarters of the way to the men's room I saw a tall, thin, bald man staring up at a TV screen. His hands were playing with a glass of gin or vodka, with two wedges of lime along the side.

I stopped for some reason. I became a bit confused, even frightened. Why were so many men drinking during the day in this ugly place? Where were their wives, children, jobs, pets, friends? Why was the place so bloody sad?

"Excuse me. Are you Dennis?"

He wheeled on his stool and stared at us. He was not young. He was carefully groomed even though his clothes were intensely tacky.

He didn't answer.

"We looked for you at the Museum Pub. We didn't know you had left there."

"Am I supposed to know you?"

"No. But you do know Timothy Prosper, don't you?"

Now he really scrutinized us. For the first time I could see that something was wrong with his right eye; it didn't focus properly.

"Never heard the name," he said, and turned away from us.

I thrust the jacket photo in front of him.

"Look! Don't tell me you don't know him. He drank in your bar for years. You served him for years."

He stared into his drink. He said nothing.

"All I want to know is why Timothy Prosper frequented the Museum Pub when he lives and works on Irving Place. It's a long way to travel."

He didn't speak. I placed a folded fifty-dollar bill on the counter near his glass.

He laughed as he picked it up. He dipped it into his drink, as if it were a stirrer. Then he said, "You're a barrel of laughs, lady. But sure, let me tell you. I think he drank there because he often stayed at a hotel around the corner. The Duvalle. Now, that makes sense, doesn't it?"

A.G. and I walked back to Madison and stationed ourselves across from the hotel.

It was one of those very small, very elegant, very expensive, and very subdued hotels just off Madison that seemed to cater to Europeans from Never-Never Land.

"Why would he stay in a place like this?" A.G. asked.

"I have no idea."

"You know, Alice, you won't find out a thing from the staff at that hotel. They don't disclose guest lists; they don't disclose anything. And you can't buy those doormen."

"I am well aware of that."

I noticed that the doorman on duty wore white gloves. I hadn't seen that in years. We stood there in the cold wind and watched for we knew not what.

"This is getting stupid, Alice. We're not getting anywhere. We're going about it all wrong."

"Impatient, A.G.?" I retorted bitterly. "Remember, it was you who persuaded us to go for the reward money. It was you who pointed out the resemblance of the gargoyles. Losing heart now? Can't stand a few setbacks, A.G.? If indeed today was a setback. In fact I don't think it was, A.G. I think we've come quite far. We know that Prosper was staying in a place he shouldn't have been staying in, for unknown but suspicious purposes. That's a good day's work, A.G. Wouldn't you agree?"

He didn't answer. He was angry. He dropped me off home in a cab and he didn't even ask to come up.

It was a good thing he didn't. Tony was waiting

for me in my loft, having used the key I'd asked him not to use again without my permission. He was fast asleep in my bed.

Tony Basillio did not awake until six that evening, and the moment he did awake, he had the effrontery to ask for a cup of coffee made from freshly ground beans.

I made him a cup of instant Medaglia d'Oro instead.

He grinned when I handed it to him.

"You look like the proverbial cat who swallowed the proverbial canary," I noted. "Perhaps you have achieved yet another one of your famous seductions."

Tony sipped his coffee. All he said in response was, "That proverbial cat died of feline gastroenteritis, Swede. One canary too many?"

He took another long sip, then put the coffee down and said, "I am not here to discuss any aspect of my social life."

"That's good. I am so bored by seduction tales about nineteen-year-old ingenues."

"In fact, Swede, I am here to discuss an interesting development in the social life of my assignment— one Timothy Prosper."

"You mean you found something?" I asked, suddenly excited.

"Well, let me put it this way . . . I persevered

and I delivered. Picture the scene, Swede. Your best surveillance man, me, standing across the street from their Irving Place digs, sipping coffee from a cart at 8 A.M. in the freezing morning. The wife exits first. I ignore her. I know my assignment. At nine o'clock the prey emerges. Frozen but faithful, I energize myself and follow the sad fool. He skirts Gramercy Park and walks uptown on Lexington. He has a buttered bagel and coffee on Lexington and Thirtieth. Then he keeps heading uptown. He stops in a magazine store. He window-shops on Madison Avenue. He goes into a bank at Fifth Avenue and 52nd Street. I am still with him, ignoring all discomforts, thinking only of you, Swede, and the poor missing child, and those poor dead geriatric lovers, and of course the few shekels that will be distributed to me from the reward money. What did that ambulance chaser say? A hundred sixty-six thousand dollars each?"

"Get to the point, Tony. Get to the bloody point."

"Don't rush me, Swede. A true surveillance expert must make a full report. Anyway, then, to my astonishment, he saunters into Central Park and walks right into the zoo. I follow, paying admission out of my own pocket, which I expect to be reimbursed for when I submit my expense report. Can you guess what Mr. Prosper does next? I doubt it. He strolls into the Penguin House. Now, everyone in New York knows that the Penguin House is the finest place in the world to cool off during a summer heat wave.

You just sit there and watch the penguins cavort behind the glass in refrigerated splendor. But in the dead of winter—only madmen enter. Ah, the mystery was solved quickly. A young woman was waiting for him—a beautiful young woman. Can you imagine that, Swede? A tryst in the Penguin House? Only a novelist could think of that. They sat down together on a bench, very, very close but not touching, and just whispered the frozen time away."

"Did you hear him mention a name?" I asked.

"No."

"What did she look like?"

"As I said, beautiful."

"Yes, but what did she look like?" I demanded, a bit frustrated.

"Black hair. Early twenties. Knockout body. Maybe green eyes, maybe gray eyes."

It was futile, I realized, to try to get a coherent description from him. Tony Basillio was, like many stage designers, virtually incapable of painting pictures with words. They needed a visual language. If you hired Tony to work on a production that required three sets, he would sound like an idiot if questioned as to his intentions. But give him a crayon and paper and in a second he would lay out a series of dazzling possibilities for each of the three sets, ranging from surreal to realistic to minimal.

I rushed about the apartment until I found a small, elegant Eileen Fisher shopping bag with plenty of white space. I gave it to him with one of my finest fat list-making pencils.

He worked for not more than five minutes and then pushed the sketch over to me.

I looked at the woman's face. If I had not been seated, I would have fallen.

"Hand me the phone," I whispered.

He complied. I called A.G. He was just going out to eat. "Forget it!" I ordered. "Get over here now! Bring a sandwich if you like. Bring anything. But come fast, A.G."

"What's going on?" Tony asked, unhappy at the prospect of socializing once again with A.G. Roth.

"Quite possibly, Tony," I said, "the queen has left the hive."

I could not sit still while waiting for A.G. to arrive. I paced the perimeter of my large loft, fending off Tony's confusion as to what was transpiring, as to why I was acting like such an idiot.

It took A.G. thirty minutes to arrive, and he did bring a sandwich. I took him by the arm and led him to that spot in the loft where the light is most bright on a dark winter evening. He sat down. I took his sandwich away from him. It smelled like Swiss cheese and mustard.

"Are you alert, A.G.?" I shouted at him. And then caught myself—I was becoming excessive.

A.G. didn't answer my alertness query. Instead, he

gave Tony a long, dirty look, as if obviously it was the stage designer's words or actions that had deranged me.

I thrust the sketch into his hands. "What is this?" he asked.

I knelt down beside him and put my hands on his thigh, almost, I suppose, in what could be construed as a loving gesture.

I asked him: "Do you know her, A.G.? Have you seen her before?"

He stared at the sketch for only a moment.

"Sure," he said matter-of-factly.

"No! No! Study it carefully!" I ordered.

He obeyed me.

"Now are you sure you've seen her before?"

"Yes. It's the girl who gave me the kittens," he said, "the actress who lived with Lila and Alex."

"You mean Asha?"

"Right."

I turned to Tony: "Please inform your colleague as to what you saw pertaining to this Asha."

He shrugged and started talking. I waited almost to the end of his narrative.

Then I could no longer contain my triumphant glee. I snatched Bushy off the sofa, held him high above my head with both hands, and commenced a peculiar synthesis of fandango and flamenco around the loft.

When I finished this nonsense, I informed Tony

and A.G.—they both looked a bit shell-shocked—that we must repair to Sam Tully's place immediately. They didn't protest.

I called Sam. He was inebriated. He craved company, he said.

Then I called Nora. No, she could not come. She was being crushed to death by a flood of tourists demanding their pre-theater dinners.

"Are you ready, gentlemen?" I asked.

They appeared to be. But not ready enough, I thought.

"You do understand what has happened, don't you? We have been vindicated beyond our wildest dreams. It is no longer merely a case of a connection between the gargoyles, the sour cream, the missing child. Not at all. These cases have merged. They are . . . it is . . . as they say . . . one enchilada."

I started to giggle at my Latina metaphor. Poor Alice. I kissed the cats good-bye and rushed out. They, the men, followed.

Sam Tully lived in a rent-controlled walk-up hovel on Spring Street, at the western edge of posh Soho.

His door was open, as usual. Sam refused to lock his door. The old mystery writer was sprawled on an incredibly derelict easy chair, smoking, without shoes or socks. The apartment was frigid because Sam always kept the windows leading to the fire escape open so that Pickles, his cat, had free access to the roof. There was even some snow on the floor.

Pickles was in the window and hissed at us as we walked in.

"You are all God's children," Sam shouted. "So sit down."

We all managed to find chairs. Pickles's hissing never let up for a second. The sudden revelation came to me that I was in an apartment with three men, and each one had at least one orphan cat as a result of the murder of said cat's owner. It was very peculiar.

Sam threw a box of cheddar cheese crackers at Tony and told him to eat.

Then I told Sam about Dennis and the Duvalle and the meeting in the Penguin House of Asha and Timothy Prosper. When I had finished, the inebriation seemed to have been squeezed out of him.

He leaned forward and spoke quietly, with great feeling, and yes, even wonderment.

"Honey, do you see what is happening? We are, maybe, about to get that little kid to reappear. And we are about to nail the slimy creep who crushed your old friends. Do you know how close we are, honey?"

He looked at all of us, one at a time, and kept repeating: "Do you know how close we are?"

Tony said: "What I'm beginning to feel is that the Baby Kate kidnapping wasn't what it seemed to be. I'm beginning to sense some ugly options. You know what I mean?"

Sam held up his hands and shouted: "Naw! Listen! That's the worst thing you can do now. Don't think. Don't speculate. Just take the next tiny little step. Like a teeny-weeny, itsy-bitsy, polka-dot bikini. Little steps. Make them smaller and smaller. Like a snail chasing a runaway car. Don't try to catch up. Just let yourself get run over."

A.G. said to me: "He's right. We have to be slow and steady now."

I knew there were all kinds of visions dancing in all kinds of heads. A hundred and sixty-six thousand dollars each. Sour cream. Speed. A little girl whom we'd never met.

"What do you suggest, Sam?" I asked.

"The bartender, honey. Get the son of a bitch. Get him to open up. When did Prosper take Asha to that hotel? How many times? When did it start? Put the screws to that Dennis. Squeeze him dry. Believe me, he knows things we need. Scare him. Put the creep on a spit and roast him in the midnight sun."

"But Sam, you told me the only way to get a bartender to talk is with money. How much is this going to cost?"

"Never listen to what I say, honey. Just watch what I do."

"You want to talk to Dennis, Sam?"

"Yeah."

"When?"

"Now, honey, now. You got cab fare?"

"We'll all go," I said.

"Hell, no!" Sam shouted. "I don't need no assistants. Seedy bars are what I do. They're my religion. Don't you know that, honey?"

"You need coffee, Sam."

"Ain't that the truth."

"I'll make you a cup. And then I'll go with you. Just you and I, Sam."

"Is that wise?" A.G. asked.

I never knew how to answer a question like that.

How odd! Earlier in the day, when A.G. and I had entered Rose's Tavern, it was packed.

Now, at nine in the evening, when Sam and I walked in, it was sparsely peopled.

We immediately went to one of the side booths. There was no waitress service. Sam went to the bar and came back with two bottles of Heineken Dark beer to share, and a Maker's Mark for himself.

"Do you see him?" he asked.

I carefully studied the ten or eleven denizens drinking at the long bar.

"I don't see him, Sam."

"Describe him again to me, honey."

"Old, tall, bald, a bad eye."

"Which eye?"

"I don't remember, Sam."

He cursed under his breath and drank his whiskey. I held a bottle of beer but didn't drink. The tavern was much darker at night, its seediness overwhelmed by an almost sinister glow.

"I've been here a dozen times, and I never liked it one bit," Sam revealed.

"Recently?"

"No, no. Maybe ten years ago."

"When I came here earlier today, they were playing Tony Bennett on the jukebox."

"You were lucky. Usually it's Sinatra—until you lie down and scream, 'No more, No more.' "

As if to prove a point, the first strains of "The Summer Wind" emerged from the jukebox.

Sam pointed to the rear of the long bar. "There used to be a steam table and a carving station there—a guy in a white hat making roast beef, corned beef, brisket sandwiches. But it was a small steam table compared to the big ones in the bars on Eighty-sixth. All gone now."

His comments degenerated into a mumble, and I let him mumble on without interruption. A full-scale Sinatra concert was now in force, supplementing Tully's mumbling. I dozed a bit but was brought up sharply when the voice changed to Willie Nelson.

The big clock over the bar read exactly 10:20 when Dennis walked in.

"That's him," I whispered urgently to Sam.

Dennis was wearing an old blue suit with a sweater under the suit jacket. No topcoat. His tie—the knot of which jutted out over the sweater—was quite old fashioned, the kind bank tellers and civil servants used to wear. He was walking a bit unsteadily, and he looked ten years older than he had earlier in the day.

He sat down about six stools from the end and ordered a drink.

Sam said: "Bring him over, honey, and then keep your mouth shut. Just do what I tell you to do."

I didn't appreciate those idiotic orders. But I did walk over to Dennis.

"You again?" he asked wearily.

"Me again."

"You got another fifty for me? Is that it? You're Mother Teresa's niece and you give away fifties."

"Someone wants to meet you," I said, pointing to the booth where Tully sat.

He didn't even look there. He shook his head. "Not interested," he said.

"I think you ought to go to the booth," I pressed. "I think it would be to your benefit; for your health; for body and soul."

"Are you threatening me, lady?"

"No, Dennis. I think you should consider me the voice of reason, particularly since it appears you are no longer employed, and barely employable."

My last comment unnerved him. He took his glass and walked to the booth, then slid in across from Sam. I sat down beside Dennis, in effect barring his exit.

Everyone looked at everyone and said nothing. Then Dennis burst out laughing, and asked, "Who the hell are you people?"

"A friend of a friend," Sam said.

"Yeah, sure."

"Why'd they fire you, Dennis?" Sam asked.

"Who says I was fired?"

"A little birdie."

"Birdies are rats with wings."

I noticed that Dennis's face was now flushed, and he was grimacing. And as he grimaced, the soft lines in his face grew to crevices. For some reason, I began to feel very, very sorry for this man.

There was an awkward, pregnant silence. Then Sam said to me: "Give him the sketch."

"I extracted Tony's art from my bag and handed it to Dennis. He refused to touch it. I placed it down in front of him on the table.

He stared at the pencil likeness of a young woman. Then he looked up: "What do you people really want from me?"

"Not much," Sam shot back. He leaned over and smoothed the edges of Tony's drawing. "When was the last time you saw her in the Museum Pub? How often did she and Prosper go to the Duvalle Hotel? What do you know about her? What do you know about her thing with Prosper?"

Dennis didn't say a word. He stared at the wood behind Sam's head.

Sam's voice got soft, almost pleading: "You'll never see us again, Denny. Sure, I can call you Denny, can't I? We'll never bug you again. Just tell us what you know. A little is good. A lot is good. Anything you got."

Dennis brought his eyes down to the sketch. He moved it a bit. He examined it.

Then he said: "I don't know her. I never saw her in my life."

Sam cursed him. Dennis winced.

Sam seemed to crouch down low in the booth, like an old psychotic snake. He started to hiss: "You know what this is all about, don't you? Prosper's kid. The kid they snatched. Well, you listen good. That case is being reopened. And if you don't open your mouth, we're going to speak to the cops and tell them you're implicated, and give them all kinds of little hints that you're a sick old bastard who gets his kicks being around little girls. Very little girls. They'll pull you in, Dennis, and they'll make your life a whole lot more miserable. Think on that."

Dennis was very pale now. The sweat was staining his shirt collar. His fingers were leaving little smudges on his glass. I felt ugly, cheap. I wished this would end.

Dennis nodded slowly, defeated.

"Christina," he said.

Sam howled at him: "What? No! Her name is Asha."

"Don't know her. Don't know any Asha. Christina.

Prosper went to the Duvalle with Christina. They used to meet in the bar. At least twice a week."

"Who the hell is Christina?" Sam shouted.

"An au pair girl, worked on 79th Street. From Finland. Tall, beautiful. So blond her hair seemed white."

Then Dennis pushed the sketch over to me and reiterated: "Never saw this girl before."

"Where is Christina now?" I asked.

"Gone."

"What do you mean, gone?"

"Went back to Finland."

"When?"

"Maybe three months ago. After she left, Prosper would have two drinks and then start crying. Two more drinks and he'd collapse, and his fat friend would have to drag him home."

Sam hit the sketch with his thumb and demanded: "But what about Asha? What about her?"

"How many times do I have to tell you? Don't know her. Never saw her."

There was a long silence. Sam closed his eyes. I stood up. Dennis slipped out of the booth and returned to the bar. He looked on the verge of collapse.

I took a long drink of the warmish beer, right from the bottle. Then I asked no one in particular: "Who is Christina? What is she?"

Sam, his eyes still closed, said wearily: "We have to do some thinking, honey."

*   *   *

The time was an hour before midnight. The place was Boots, Sam's bar south of Canal Street, the place where he goes when he needs to think—when he wants to philosophize. Sam believes that coherent thinking can take place only in a bar.

I loathed and feared Boots. It made Rose's Tavern look like the Oak Room at the Plaza. But I went there with him out of necessity and solidarity. Let's face it—we now had a philosophical problem called Christina.

Boots was, as usual, filled with non-mingling, often menacing cliques. There was a black clique, an Hispanic clique, a gay hustler clique, and a white thug group. Each had its own set of tables in the rear. Only the bar itself was nonspecific, and that was where we sat.

The jukebox was playing Joe Cocker.

After Sam had ordered his drink, he said to me: "Make your call, honey."

I knew exactly what he meant. I threaded my way between the cliques to the pay phone in the rear and called A.G. I asked him—ordered would be a better term—to go through his Baby Kate files and find a name . . . find anything about a young Finnish au pair named Christina.

A.G., in his gentlemanly way, replied, with four questions, to wit:

—Where was I now

—Would I spend the night with him

—Did Dennis the bartender give me Christina's name

—Could he begin his search of the files in the morning

The only question I answered was the last one: "No! Now!"

I waited for ten minutes at the pay phone, feeding it. A.G. came back on and said, "Nothing."

"Thank you."

I hung up and returned to the bar. Sam was staring at his face in the wall mirror.

"Nothing?" he asked.

"Exactly."

I sat down on the stool and stared at myself in the mirror. I was drinking club soda. He was drinking more bourbon.

He said: "I was wondering how it felt when the speed started working on their bodies and heads. Did they just feel everything getting louder and faster? Do you know what I mean? The head pounding. The eyes hurting. The brain beginning to go like Tito Puente."

"You're getting morbid, Sam," I replied, wincing. Oh, that bloody sour cream and mushrooms.

Joe Cocker went off the jukebox. On came Jerry Lee Lewis with "A Whole Lotta Shakin' Going On." I wished to be out of there. How miserable I felt.

"You know, Sam," I noted, "we did a very ugly little dance uptown."

"You mean putting the screws on Dennis."

"Yes."

"Had to be done. And it worked."

"Yes, it did. At least he gave us a name that might be important. But it was a very ugly scene. And I don't know why it worked. Do you really think he's a child molester?"

"Hell, no! Where do you come from, honey? Never-Never Land? He got scared because there's a whole lot of people in the world who don't like being picked up by cops. Particularly people who lost their last job because they dipped into the till."

"You don't know that about Dennis."

"Look, honey, no one fires a bartender in a bar like that after fifteen years unless the guy started pocketing the receipts."

Suddenly he pointed to his image in the mirror across the bar.

"You know, I'm getting ugly," he noted. "I figure you find this hard to believe, but at one time I wasn't a bad-looking guy."

I didn't comment.

He swivelled on his stool and faced me. "What's going on with those two characters?"

"Who?" I asked.

"Basillio and the lawyer."

"What do you mean?"

"You sleeping with both of them?"

"None of them."

110

"You read my *Only the Dead Wear Socks*, didn't you? Remember what Harry Bondo said about tall, good-looking women who are moving on a bit, age-wise?"

"Not really."

"Bondo said: 'They got thorns on their toes.' "

I had no idea what that meant. I wasn't interested. My eyelids were beginning to feel like frying pans. I said: "We're here to think about Christina, Sam."

"Right."

"You have any thoughts?"

"It's early."

"What do we do next?"

"But honey, that's your job. You propose, I dispose."

"The fact is, Sam, the more we look, the more the thing expands."

He grunted. Then he rubbed his hands together and looked at them. "So maybe," he said, "it's time to forget the physics of the mess and go to the humanity of it."

Jerry Lee Lewis went off. Sarah Vaughn came on.

The humanity of it? I was bothered by his phrase. Bothered and interested.

"Go ahead, Sam."

He ordered another drink and lit a cigarette. He blew the smoke upward.

"Think, honey. What do you remember about our little talk with Dennis?"

"A number of things, Sam. His fear. The way the

name Christina popped out. His dogged refusal to recognize the woman in the sketch. My chagrin that instead of confirming a criminal conspiracy between Asha and Prosper, all we got was a brand-new problem."

"Yeah, yeah, honey. But what do you remember as Alice Nestleton, the actress, the woman who could go deep into a part and come up with images and speech that tear at your heart? Yeah, that! You know what I mean?"

I sat and thought for a long time. Then I said: "It would have to be when Dennis was describing how Prosper, mourning his lost love and drinking himself into oblivion, was dragged home by his faithful friend."

"And who was his friend, honey?"

"Well, I guess it was that NYU professor—Porter Whatshisname."

Sam grinned. "The fat man, you mean."

That's how it was that we knew where to go the next morning.

Chapter 11

I remembered his full, exact name the moment I saw him again. Sam and I found Porter Boudreau seated happily at the desk in the anteroom, opening mail. It was not quite eleven in the morning. The student we had encountered before was not in sight.

Professor Boudreau was dressed a bit less flamboyantly this time, in a dark blue flannel shirt with a darker blue tie and light blue suspenders. Behind the desk, his weight seemed to anchor him—like an obese gargoyle with a friendly disposition.

There was a thermos of coffee on top of the desk from which he drank huge drafts as he haphazardly slit open the mail with a heavy metal letter opener.

Judging by the smirk on his lips, he found our reappearance to be quite amusing. "I knew beyond a shadow of a doubt that you would return quickly. And how did I know? Ah, because you are both mysterious angels of mercy; you wander the earth doing justice, loving mercy, walking humbly with your gods, and trying to help Timothy Prosper even though he doesn't give a damn about you or your help. At least, that's what you claim, isn't it? Missions of mercy."

He slit open another envelope and began to peruse the contents.

"Have you seen Timothy Prosper lately?" I asked pleasantly.

"No."

"Have you see Christina lately?" I followed up, innocently, searching for an inappropriate response from him.

No shadow crossed his face. He kept studying the letter while he asked, equally innocently: "And who might this Christina be?"

Continuing the chess game, if it was that, I answered his question with another question.

"When was the last time you saw Prosper?"

"I told you on your last tedious visit. A while ago. The poor man's in a depression. He suffers them periodically, ever since his child vanished."

Sam spoke for the first time.

"I think the last time you saw him was when you dragged the drunken fool out of the Museum Pub and got him home. That's what Dennis seems to think. And you know bartenders. They got good memories. They got claws in their memory boxes. They fasten on drunks and their friends."

The large man seemed to ignore Sam's comment. He snapped one of his suspenders and held up the letter he was reading. "Now, this is very sad," he announced. "A letter from a poet in Kentucky. He wants to know how to apply for the Writers in Residence program here. But I don't take poets anymore. I have begun to loathe poets. Too much facility with language. Too much subterfuge. I have become a prose missionary in my old age. I prefer clunky writers—novelists who struggle to put one phrase after another in declarative sentences. Like Timothy. Now, let's face it, he's a fine novelist. But he has little command of the English language. Wouldn't you say so? One day I shall write a very important essay—even more important than my Yates/Mussolini/Leda/Swan revelations. It will be about the literature of Clunk. But I shall spell it with a 'k'—to give it philosophical panache. Yes! Klunk, with a 'K.' What say you, angels of mercy?"

He flung the poet's letter aside and began to open another one.

Sam was furious. He started to say something ugly. I shut him up with a gesture. I signaled that this would be my show. He shrugged, skeptical.

"You had better start taking us seriously, Professor Boudreau."

"But I do, my love," Boudreau replied, smiling.

"Because, let me inform you, your friend Timothy Prosper is now a suspect in a murder investigation."

"You're jesting."

"No, I'm not. I believe—and the police will soon believe—that he participated in the gruesome murder of a man and his wife."

"And when did this happen?"

"A very short time ago."

"No doubt that is why he is avoiding me. No doubt poor Tim is still washing the blood off his AK-47. You know how sloppy those things get."

"This is no joke. You too are implicated."

"Oh, come now."

"You're in it almost as deep as he is. Now tell me what you know about Christina."

He exploded in anger. "I don't know a solitary thing about that stupid Finnish bitch."

"But you've met her, haven't you?"

He seemed to be weighing the consequences of further denial. "Of course," he finally said.

"In the Museum Pub?"

"Yes."

"Once? Twice? Many times?"

"Many times."

"And you know that she and Prosper were lovers?"

He burst out laughing.

"What's so funny? The man seems to have loved

her greatly. Dennis told us that when she went back home, your friend fell apart. You should know. You took him home all the time."

"Like most bogus angels of mercy, you're too naive to cause any trouble whatsoever."

"How am I naive?"

"Tim loved every woman he ever bought. He even loved his wife."

"What are you talking about? Bought? Hardly. His wife has the money, not him."

"There are other mediums of exchange."

"You mean he bought Christina too?"

"Of course. But with old-fashioned money. Her rate was, if I remember, six hundred dollars a night for all the love you could harvest."

"Are you telling me that Christina is a prostitute?"

"Yes."

I felt very stupid now, very unsure of myself.

"Did he often frequent prostitutes?" I asked.

"He lived for them."

"I find that very hard to believe," I replied. I looked at Sam. He was grinning evilly. He would be. After all, his fictional detective, Harry Bondo, was a notoriously frequent visitor to very seamy Chinatown brothels.

"My dear golden-haired matron, I truly believe that Tim would not pay more than three hundred a night for you—but pay he would. Don't you understand? He is one of those men who only enjoy purchased favors—purchased, funky, anonymous sex. Oh, it's too complex, too idiosyncratic, too furtive a syndrome to even speak about coherently. And those of us who do not suffer from it can never appreciate it. At least, let us be compassionate."

"Asha!" I blurted out.

"Who?"

"Did he ever buy love from a young woman named Asha?"

"Names are not my strong point. Concepts!"

He returned to the letters on his desk.

The can of worms had sprung open. Now we would have to deal with the churning mess. Sam and I walked out. The snowflakes were falling again. Furtive, furtive, furtive. I've always loved the sound of that word.

It could be described, I suppose, as a War Council of the Cat People.

It took place about thirty-six hours after Porter Boudreau revealed the particulars of Prosper's psyche—at least in his relationships with women.

The troops—A.G., Sam Tully, Nora, Basillio, and I—gathered at A.G.'s apartment at four in the afternoon. Cocktail hour, sort of, or high tea if you stretched the point. In any case, none of us would have turned down a little snack and something to drink. A.G. served potato chips, which was a bit embarrassing. Of course everyone knew that A.G.'s law practice had collapsed in the late 1980s. He had never been able to get back on his feet, much less join that circle of lawyers who now represent actors, producers, writers, et al.— entertainment law or intellectual property law as that niche was called—and make a great deal of money.

But even down-and-out lawyers like A.G. have to do better than potato chips.

A.G.'s bad hosting did not end with the chips. No, it got much worse than that. After Sam and I laid out the situation to the assembled, A.G. began to rhapsodize about the kittens, Billy and Bob, who were scampering from one visitor to another, begging for love.

Granted, kittens are startling, endearing, adorable things. Too much so to describe in words. It is best to keep silent about their startling, endearing, adorable qualities and simply observe and enjoy them. A.G., however, could not be quiet. He was discoursing endlessly about the little critters, and making me really uncomfortable. But cat people solidarity forced us to listen as he described their lovable antics.

Nora was the lone holdout; she was distinctly not a cat person. And so she was the logical one to shut him up—and, luckily, she did.

"I suppose," she interrupted, "we're here to figure out what to do next. If anything. I mean, given what you told us, Alice, I think it's time to drop the damn thing. It's gotten too muddy, too morbid. Don't we pay the cops to deal with things like this?"

And that's when Tony Basillio stepped out of character. Maybe, after what he had heard from Sam and me, he saw his $166,000 share in the Baby Kate retrieval slipping out of his grasp. Maybe he had told the young thing he was currently enamored of that he would shortly be affluent. Maybe some other pressing need was motivating him to go after the money—who knows?—but he made a startling presentation.

Seated on A.G.'s piano stool, he launched into his spiel. He spoke with intensity, but his words were oddly free of his usual rancor toward A.G. or Sam or me or Nora or anyone. What I heard instead was a cosmic rancor toward Timothy Prosper.

Let me reproduce it:

"The way I see it, our friend Timothy is pathological. A nutcase. And I think he pays this Asha to introduce him to young actresses who'll turn a few tricks to pay the rent. But so what, you say? Would that be so bad? So evil? No. Not if he had stopped at that; then he'd just be a garden-variety cheating husband, a run-of-the-mill nutcase. Hell, all writers are. But he didn't stop. I think he conspired with Asha to murder Alex and Lila. Why? I haven't the foggiest idea.

"Even so, that's only the beginning of his insanity.

I do think that Timothy Prosper, sick bastard that he is, conspired in the kidnapping of his own child. For the ransom money. Don't ask me for the particulars. I don't know them. Don't ask me for evidence. I don't have any. Believe me, though, this Prosper is evil and crazy and the only way to find out what went down is to trap him, panic him, sweat him."

An astonished silence greeted Tony's outburst. A.G. was the first to break that silence. He asked in a very calm voice: "Assuming that your intuition about Prosper has some correspondence to reality—and assuming that he would crack if trapped, panicked, and sweated—how do we go about doing that without kidnapping him?"

"I have no idea," Tony replied.

Tully leaned over and whispered to me: "Well, honey, do your stuff."

I looked around the room. They were waiting for me, I realized. They were obviously all in unanimity with Tony's views—more or less—and waiting for the Cat Woman to design the trap.

I am not bragging, but the idea came to me literally in seconds.

Rent a hotel room.

Send a card to Prosper from Christina saying that she was back in the U.S. and wanted him to come to her hotel room for the usual transaction.

Once he stepped into the room, he would find not the nubile Christina but a pair of determined interrogators who would threaten him with disclosure . . . trip him up by citing Asha's nonexistent confession, which implicated him in murder and kidnapping . . . and menace him with talk of gargoyles, the fires of hell, and anything else we could think of.

I articulated it.

There was applause. Except from Nora, who had the sense to ask: "What if he's not interested in Christina anymore?"

I replied: "Then we lose two hundred dollars."

Tony corrected me: "No, we lose a hundred sixty-six thousand dollars each."

The preparations did not go easily.

First, A.G. began to waffle. He speculated that what we were doing might leave us open to a lawsuit. It was a possible case of entrapment with intent to do emotional harm. And if the interrogation became heated, there was the possibility of a suit by Timothy Prosper on the grounds of menacing.

We dispensed with these arguments quickly on the grounds of "clear and present danger" to future victims of Prosper. The guy was a menace; we could menace him to our hearts' content.

We then proceeded to the problem of the hotel. To where should we lure him? The Duvalle was out. The staff knew both Christina and Timothy.

In fact, any place in the area of the Museum Pub, the Duvalle, or the house where Christina had worked was out of bounds, for a variety of reasons. Chance was one. Prosper could meet someone on the way to the assignation who knew Christina—perhaps had spoken to her the day before, and would express disbelief that Christina had returned to the U.S. Better to be safe than sorry.

So, after much conversation we settled on a businessman's hotel on East 34th Street between Lexington and Third—the Du Pont.

It was only fifteen short blocks away from the Prosper domicile.

As to the nature of the note—everyone had his or her own idea.

Nora, in fact, didn't want a note at all. She suggested a telephone call to Prosper; the caller should identify himself or herself as a friend of Christina's and pass on her request.

Sam wanted a postcard: cryptic, short, tight—just a place, date, and time of assignation.

There was a great deal of give-and-take discussion.

We decided on half a sheet of white bond paper inserted into a small white stamped envelope.

It would be addressed to *Professor* Timothy Prosper, as if it had been sent by an academic colleague or a student.

It would be mailed to his home.

The typed note itself would read simply, BACK IN THE U.S. WITH FRIEND, CARLA. THE DU PONT. 34TH AND LEXINGTON. ROOM ? 9 P.M. THURSDAY.

We wouldn't sign the note. That would be too risky. Christina and Timothy might have some pet names for each other. We couldn't even use a salutation, for the same reason.

And the friend, "Carla," had to be put in because Timothy would most likely ask the clerk to call room ? from the desk, informing either Christina or Carla that he was downstairs.

Carla would then answer and tell the clerk to send him up.

The note would be dispatched on Saturday and most likely reach Prosper Monday or Tuesday.

The final element in the plot was the identity of my colleague in the hotel room.

Sam suggested that the interrogation be conducted *àla* NYPD: classic good cop/bad cop. I, he said, should conduct the interrogation and be fierce. A.G., he suggested, should be my companion—the good cop—on the grounds that he had a mellifluous way of speaking.

Nora objected and, gritting her teeth, recommended Tony as my colleague in the hotel room.

She said, and this is a direct quote: "Take Basillio. There may be trouble. If this guy is really a nutcase, there has to be trouble. He's going to be very unhappy. Right? So Basillio has to be there. Because, like it or not, he is the only one of us in some kind of physical shape. Alice doesn't need an assistant in that hotel room. I think she needs a bodyguard."

Her logic was impeccable. Tony would accompany me.

So that was that. I made a reservation for two at the Du Pont. Two hundred dollars for the night, double occupancy, under the names Tony and Carla Murray, arriving Thursday afternoon and checking out Friday morning. I requested a room number now. They gave me 601. I typed the note. I mailed it.

We had no guarantee that Prosper would show. But obsessional characters usually act in character. Don't they?

We checked in at three-forty in the afternoon. The desk clerk confirmed that Room 601 was waiting for us. I paid cash, in advance. Not that I was required to do so; all I had to do was present my credit card—the sole remaining one out of what I recalled as hundreds of credit cards issued promiscuously to me in the boom-and-bust 1980s. But I couldn't do that because the name Carla Murray was nowhere to be found on said card.

This payment of cash made the individual behind the elegantly minimalist counter a bit edgy. But he handed over the key anyway. I guess he decided I did not look like a drug or hot stock courier, although I was dressed a bit flamboyantly.

I had not worn the green wool pants suit in six years or so. It was a tight fight, since I had gained a few pounds in the interim.

Tony was wearing one of his theater people out-fits—jeans, a sport jacket over a sweatshirt, with a muffler. He looked exactly like what he was—a middle-aged, rakish, bohemian manqué. Bless him and his kind.

The elderly bellhop wore an ID tag on his breast pocket—the name sounded Portuguese. He handled our two small carry-alls elegantly and efficiently, as if we were truly players in some merger deal.

As the elevator ascended, reality began to set in. I became a bit frightened—and skeptical about our chances of pulling off this trap.

When we were ensconced in the room, which was quite nice, Basillio and I exchanged "What are we doing here?" glances.

We sat down on the sofa, a cushion apart, and stared straight ahead.

"Five hours," Tony said.

"More or less," I replied.

"Should I turn down the heat?"

"By all means."

He adjusted the apparatus on the window and then sat back down.

"You know, Swede, you and I have had our prob-lems in the past. I mean, concerning my alleged infi-delities. But know one thing! I have never frequented prostitutes."

"How nice!" I laid the sarcasm on.

Unfortunately, it infuriated him. He jumped up

and began to pace and mutter. This room—and our plan—had obviously put him as much on edge as I was. And why not? It was problematic, dangerous, and just on the cusp of legality.

"Tony, I can't hear a word you're saying," I noted pleasantly.

He wheeled. "I was saying that I never met an actress who didn't prostitute herself one way or another."

Whooooa! It was time for me to take a little stroll. So I waved ta-ta and took a walk up Lexington. I came back an hour later with a ham-and-cheese sandwich for Tony and a chicken-salad sandwich for myself.

We munched in silence. We both watched the clock. At six, Tony turned on a cable station and we watched, without sound, an old Hollywood black-and-white movie called *The Lusty Men*, with Robert Mitchum, Susan Hayward, and Arthur Kennedy. It seemed to be about rodeo cowboys.

We never switched on the lamps in the room—the only light came from the small bathroom fixture over the sink.

It was oddly pleasant there, until I began, for some reason, to think about Alex and Lila. I wanted them to know where I was . . . what I was doing. I wanted them to know that I would . . . what? . . . avenge their deaths? Of course not.

The idea of vengeance or retribution or even aggressive justice was alien to those wonderful old people. They had been kindly and fatalistic. They did nothing in broad or intense terms. They acted when they could. They helped people out. They tried to cultivate talent in an old-fashioned, European way.

But the more I thought about their pacific mode of life, the more violent I felt toward the man we were waiting for.

The movie ended. Tony asked if I wanted to play cards. I said, "Sure." But we had no deck. So we sat in silence again, except for interludes of Tony humming. I couldn't pick up the tune, but it seemed Cole Porterish.

At eight-thirty he asked, "Do you have a plan if he shows?"

"Yes," I replied, "and it's very simple. Hit him with Asha, from the beginning. Stick to our story: Asha has seen the light. Asha has confessed all. Asha has put him right in the middle of the double murder and the kidnapping."

"He'll think we're cops," Tony said.

"No. Maybe from the D.A.'s office."

"We should have a tape running."

"It's too late now."

"I'm beginning to get a little uncomfortable now, Swede."

"So I noticed."

"Maybe we should have tried to contact him again."

"But you yourself said he's a nutcase. And we all

agreed, Tony. The man is disturbed. Whether or not he is using Asha to procure women . . . whether or not he orchestrated the murder and the kidnapping . . . whether or not he sent the gargoyle poster—the man is disturbed and implicated. We don't know what he did, or how much he did, but he surely did something. Didn't he, Tony? And you and I know that never in a million years would the NYPD do what we're doing now. Am I right, Tony?"

"Yes."

"And if anyone is bad in this whole mess, it's Timothy Prosper. Right, Tony?"

"Yes. Very bad."

"So now that you're getting cold feet—a bit late in the game—maybe you have a better way to proceed. Do you?"

"No."

"Do you have another option? Talk to me, Tony."

"I suppose we could just walk away."

"I'm not going to do that now. Am I, Tony?"

"No, you're not, Swede. Which is why I love you."

Tony started humming again.

"If he believes our story about Asha," I noted, "he must give a counter-story. To protect himself. He must take himself out of the center of the cyclone and onto the periphery. I would do that if I were him. Even though the periphery is incriminatory. Yes, I would do that if I were in his shoes. Wouldn't you, Tony?"

All he said in reply was: "As I told you before, Swede, I do eat mushrooms, but never in sour cream, and never fried in butter."

Tony flipped on the TV again. This time we watched an hour-long fashion show, again without turning up the sound.

At nine-twenty the phone rang. Once. Twice.

On the third ring I picked it up. "Yes?" My voice was hoarse, wooden. It was the tension, no doubt, that accounted for the strange way I sounded.

The desk clerk announced that "Tim" was there to see Christina. "Send him up," I said. I let the receiver down.

"He's on his way up," I announced to Tony.

We followed our plan. Tony went into the bathroom. He was not to emerge until Prosper and I were into it.

Once the bathroom door was closed, I stationed myself a few feet from it and waited. The curtain was going up and, as usual, I was bloody nervous.

The knock at the door unnerved me even more. He had arrived so fast. It seemed like only ten seconds since the call from the desk clerk.

I opened the door. Prosper was standing there, completely at ease—casual. Casual in his dress and equally casual in his posture. There was an almost sublime expression on his face.

"Are you Carla?" he asked.

"Yes!" I almost spat it out. His smile widened. Apparently my discomfort amused him.

Timothy Prosper was shorter, heavier, and older than the photo on his book jacket had led me to expect.

I swung the door open and he walked inside. He stared for a moment at the television we had not turned off.

Finally he asked, smiling, "Where is she?"

Tony walked into the room.

"She won't be here," I said.

He stared at me. Then at Tony.

"Am I supposed to know you people?"

"Yes," I said. "Through Asha."

The blood seemed to drain from his face. He moved to the door too quickly for either of us, and opened it.

But he never got outside.

A figure was blocking his exit. He stepped back into the room, no longer Mr. Casual—he was highly agitated.

The figure joined us. It was a woman, wearing a green felt hat.

She raised her right arm and aimed the gun she was holding at Timothy Prosper's face. She fired twice. He dropped to the floor. She walked over to his body and fired five more shots into him. The fine hotel rug was a marsh of blood and gore.

Chapter 12

I was not among strangers. But then, you couldn't call NYPD detectives Campion, Greco, and Fontana friends. Of course, A.G. Roth was there by my side. He had replaced Tony after Tony was interrogated and sent home.

The walls of the station house were a bright green.

The detectives were seated on one side of the long table, A.G. and I on the other side. It was ten hours after the newest horror . . . the morning hours of the new day.

Detective Campion was berating me. I kept trying to remember her first name—was it Luann?

"Cat Woman? Is that the nickname they gave you? A better one would be the Black Tulip . . . or was it a gardenia? Oh, well, you know what I mean. The angel of death. *Comprende?*"

A.G. said wearily: "Is this necessary?"

"Not really," she replied. "But after all, counselor, shouldn't we marvel that your client, if she is your client, is now responsible for the deaths of three people because she likes cute edibles as gifts . . . and another person because she's involved in some kind of anti-hooker moral crusade. I mean, if we can't marvel at all of this—what can we marvel at?"

Silence. Neither A.G. nor I knew what to say in response.

Detective Campion continued, but in a much less emotional tone.

"I could easily charge you, arrest you, and convict you, Miss Nestleton. I would do so happily. But the punishment would not in any way approximate the consequences of your misdemeanors. Besides, maybe we should be thankful to you. After all, you did catch a killer. Or rather, you staged a killing and both victim and murderer followed the script."

"The script was not for murder!" I said.

"Well, that's the way it turned out, didn't it?"

"I had no idea his wife would show up."

"No, you probably didn't."

"Why did she kill him?"

"You really want to know, Miss Nestleton?"

"Yes."

"Of course you do. And I am obliged to tell you. Because, in a strange, perverted way, your inquiries have proved invaluable to those of us on the Baby Kate case. You didn't know what you were doing.

But neither did anyone else. Listen carefully. I will tell you only once. Of course, what I'm telling you comes from Hannah Prosper's mouth, and from the mouths of killers often comes idiocy."

She gestured to the two homicide detectives. "Do you want to get some coffee?" Greco nodded. Campion said nothing until he returned and set the containers down on the long table along with a handful of packets containing sugar and nondairy creamer and a few wooden stirring sticks.

We all partook, silently and sloppily.

Luann Campion began her astonishing narrative of Hannah Prosper's confession. It was much more, it seemed, than a mere confession of murder.

"It appears that Hannah found out early on in the marriage that Timothy was addicted to the company of prostitutes. But she treated him as if he was a sick child. When she became pregnant, he swore fidelity. He lied. And he infected her with gonorrhea. She almost lost the baby. But things turned around. Mother and baby began to flourish. The child Kate became Timothy's new obsession. He became an outstanding father . . . he loved her to pieces. So life became very sweet for Hannah.

"But then the addiction reasserted itself. Timothy reassumed his M.O. This time, Hannah took a ferocious revenge. They had been using a baby-sitter named Frankie Arkette, whom they had met one night at the Red Witch. They went once and only once, but they found that young waitress to be endearing and they obtained her name and home number from the old couple who owned the restaurant. Baby Kate loved Frankie. Frankie loved Baby Kate. Neither of them knew what was about to occur.

"Hannah's sick vengeance was this: She decided to stage a kidnapping of Baby Kate to teach Timothy a lesson . . . to scare him beyond his wildest dreams . . . to punish him by taking away the thing he loved most. It was not the act of a rational woman. Luckily for Hannah's vengeful plot, Frankie Arkette agreed to help once she was approached. Her motive is and was obscure. They staged a fake kidnapping. They paid a ransom. The child was supposed to be returned with the lesson learned . . . the wife's vengeance tempered with love.

"No. It didn't work that way. Frankie Arkette vanished with the child and the money. Hannah never told her husband what had really happened. But she did tell him that she believed Lila knew where the child and the baby-sitter were. The Prospers began to send bizarre threatening notes to the old couple. The gargoyle and kitten poster was just one example. They hired a young woman named Asha to insinuate herself into Lila's household and report what she saw. This Asha met with Timothy often.

"As time passed, with no sign of the child, Hannah slipped deeper and deeper into impotent fury and depression. Only one thing probably kept her alive now—Timothy had finally come to his senses about prostitutes. He had become the faithful helper of a grieving wife and mother. Or so it seemed.

"Then she found the note enticing him to the Du Pont. She followed him and happily shot him to death. Mrs. Prosper is now on suicide watch."

It was the most horrendous marriage story I had ever heard. Two sick people in a perverted *folie à deux* that ultimately destroyed their family.

A.G. leaned across the table and asked Detective Campion: "Then it was Asha who murdered the couple, wasn't it? On Hannah's orders?"

Detective Campion didn't answer. With a hand gesture, she deferred to her colleagues from Homicide.

Greco said: "We don't think so. She denies it."

A.G. exploded. "Who cares what that maniac denies! The logic is there."

Fontana replied suavely: "First of all, Hannah Prosper is past caring about what happens to her. She wants to die. She wants no more lies. She repeatedly denied ordering or participating in the couple's death. She had no idea how they died. And your logic is off base—way off. Hannah believed that Lila and Alex knew where Frankie Arkette and the child were. Why would she murder the only people who had the knowledge, she believed, to help her regain her child? Of course her belief in the old couple's knowledge of the child's whereabouts was delusional. But Hannah didn't know her life was delusional. She would not have had them killed. Never."

A.G. shut up. Greco twirled his coffee cup. The sight was painful to me. Don't ask me why. I shut my eyes. Fontana was right. Hannah Prosper was past lying. Now I too realized that Asha could not have killed Lila and Max.

It was Asha who gave me the gargoyle poster to begin with. She would never have done that if she had murdered the old couple. Telling me about that poster implicated her, I realized, because she was working for the ones who had sent the poster—the Prospers. There was no way Asha would start a chain of connections like that if she were guilty of the murders. No, it had to be Asha's way of saying that she had had nothing to do with the killings . . . and she wanted to help find the murderer . . . whoever that might be . . . no matter how it implicated her. Had the police not made it so clear that she was a suspect, no doubt she would have given the poster to them rather than to me. Clearly I didn't think she was guilty, so she thought I was safer. And perhaps she thought I was smarter than the NYPD. Perhaps.

I heard Greco say: "We are developing an alternative theory."

A.G. asked: "Which is?"

"Suicide."

"What?"

"You heard me, counselor."

"Whose suicide?"

"The couple's."

"It's an odd way to kill oneself."

"Why?"

"Because amphetamines are very unpredictable, as you well know."

I heard Fontana pick up the thread.

"They were old, weary, sedentary people—stroke- and cardiac-prone. In a way it makes spectacular sense. They didn't nod off with a hundred downers—they blew themselves away. Dramatic as hell! After all, they were actors, weren't they?"

I suddenly found this whole thing very funny. I started to laugh. Louder and louder. I had a dim sense that I was losing control, that I was going into old-fashioned hysteria.

"Get her out of here!" someone said to A.G.

A.G. took me home. I fed the cats, took two aspirin, and went to sleep. At three in the afternoon, we went to his apartment and made our calls.

By 7 P.M. all, except Nora, were assembled for the wake.

And a wake it was.

A.G. recounted the horrendous tale of the rise, fall, and death of the Prosper marriage. And Fontana's theory that Hannah Prosper's denial of involvement in the amphetamine deaths must be believed. And the new NYPD theory: that Alex and Lila had suicided.

Tony and Sam listened in silence. I barely listened at all. One of the kittens—it may have been Billy—was playing on my right knee, attacking it, clawing it, then somersaulting off it and onto my lap.

"It sounds ugly as hell. But it could have been worse," Sam said. "I mean, she was no Medea."

Tony pointed his finger at A.G. "You're not saying anything about the money. Do we get it or don't we?"

"I don't see any possibility at all," A.G. replied.

Tony shouted: "The woman orchestrated her own kid's kidnapping. We're the ones who laid that in the cops' laps."

The second kitten joined the first one on my knee. They got into a mock fight. I remembered poor old Lila on the floor in her bedroom, playing like a child with these kittens. Bob leapt up on my shoulder. He tried to hiss at his brother. It sounded like a squeal.

I heard A.G. say: "The reward is payable only if the child is recovered. Dead or alive. *Recovered.*"

"The lawyer has a point," Tully said.

Tony cursed and—maybe accidentally, maybe not—kicked over a pile of A.G.'s research papers.

I pulled one of Kitten Billy's ears gently. It was odd, I thought, how all this death had begun with that bucolic scene between the old lady and the kittens. It was that scene which had affected me so strongly as to begin the chain of sentiment that led me to purchase that gift of a meal.

And it was the kitten poster with the gargoyle that had started the investigation of the Baby Kate kidnapping.

That idiotic poster, which Hannah had sent Lila as a threat!

What was the threat? Hard to say. Just general menace? Perhaps. Or the threat that the kittens would become gargoyles—stone cold, dead, and grotesque? Perhaps.

The other kitten wanted some ear-pulling also.

Why was I beginning to obsess over the kittens now? Just to forget the horror of the last twenty-four hours?

A.G. said: "The problem is, what do we do now?"

"Nothing. This thing is over," Sam said. "It's all over."

"Bye-bye, hundred and sixty-six thousand bucks," Tony said.

It dawned on me that these people never really knew or loved Lila and Alex. They had helped me because I was a suspect, and because the deaths had led to the Baby Kate case.

"There's plenty more to do," I said. "Particularly now that those detectives are calling it a possible double suicide."

"Honey," said Sam, "they're only talking that way

because they ran out of leads. They got nowhere to go. We got nowhere to go."

"On the contrary," I said testily. "It has suddenly occurred to me that I do have somewhere to go."

"To a shrink," quipped Tony.

I ignored him. I was quiet. The kittens had vanished.

"Tell us what you're thinking," A.G. said. "What suddenly occurred to you?"

"The kittens."

"The kittens?"

"Sooner or later," Basillio said sardonically, "we always end up back with the damn cats. It's bad enough she keeps distributing feline orphans to us. But it never stops there. Oh, no. Sooner or later everything is cat-o-centric."

"Honey," Sam said, "level with us. Is that what you're thinking? That someone doped up that sour cream because of those cats?"

"Yes. I'm afraid that is what I'm thinking. But all I'm saying is that we ought to look into the matter."

A.G. retorted gently, as if I were an idiot child: "But Alice, that kitten poster with the gargoyle was just a way for psychotic Hannah Prosper to keep pressure on the old woman. Billy and Bob have nothing to do with anything."

"Your conclusion, A.G., does not follow from your premise."

"Then let's get back to basics. The kittens weren't stolen, kidnapped, abused . . ."

"No, they weren't."

"So tell me," A.G. pleaded, "what you have in mind. Concretely, that is. I mean, what kind of investigation are you talking about?"

"What I mean? I mean talking to Asha . . . finding out about the other so-called threats . . . talking to the people who gave her the kittens . . . it was an animal shelter in Queens . . . talking to the party guests about the kittens. There's a whole lot to do. Believe me."

Tully got up, circumnavigated the room, lit a cigarette, and then came close to me, draping his right arm over my shoulder.

"Listen, honey. You know, you just saw a man get his brains blown out. Not a pretty sight. I think maybe you ought to cool it awhile. Your head is in a different place now. Let it get back to normal. Don't do no thinking. Relax. Drink some tea and brandy. Sleep a lot. Listen to music. Play in the snow. You get my drift?"

I threw his arm off me angrily and stood up.

"Are you people going to help me on this? Yes or no?"

Their silence was deafening.

"Yes, I'm agitated!" I shouted. "Yes! Tony and I experienced a dreadful horror. So what? Those old people are still in the grave. And I was one of the idiots who put them there. But there were others. Not idiots—killers. Get this through your heads. I'm not going to play it as it lays. Do you hear me?"

Their silence persisted. A.G. shook his head sadly.

"A pox on you all!" I shouted.

It had been a long time since I cursed anyone. And I couldn't even recall the last time I had used such archaic language.

I walked out alone. I went home alone.

Chapter 13

I woke at 9 A.M., very late for me. The loft was freezing. There was no sun. Bushy was seated at the end of the bed staring at me, sphinxlike. I wondered why he was not agitating for his breakfast.

Stump-tail Pancho was leaping obsessively from window ledge to window ledge, chasing pigeons that were not there.

"Are you playing one of your games with me?" I asked Bushy.

He didn't respond. Not even a blink. It was obvious he was challenging me to a staring contest. I decided to take him on. It was too cold to get up anyway.

I stared back. The game commenced. Fierce glares. Unswerving. Once or twice he moved one of his ears, trying to get me off balance, to break my concentration.

I was losing, I realized. The way to win at this game was not to stare into the beast's eyes—rather, stare at the whole head, widen your gaze.

But I found myself unable to widen. On the contrary, I was narrowing, boring into the geographical center of his orbs.

I dropped my eyes, exhausted. He grinned his Maine coon cat grin. I kicked him off the bed. Then, ashamed of myself, I prepared their breakfasts and crawled back into the bed with my phone.

I looked at my ceiling. It was beginning to peel.

A great sadness seemed to be enveloping me. It was coming from my toes, crawling up my body.

It wasn't one of those garden-variety depressions that afflict out-of-work actresses every other day. No. I knew what this one was about.

I had been abandoned. By A.G. and Tony and Sam Tully.

They had scoffed at my kitten thesis.

They had refused to help me reopen the investigation.

They had been revealed as traitors.

What was it? Did they really believe I was an hysterical cat-sitter who, when faced with a difficult problem, always ended up bringing cats into the equation because I didn't know what else to do?

Did they really think that when push came to shove I was a flake? Silly, disturbing word, that— flake. Did it come from peeling paint?

Oh, they thought I was a fine actress, of course . . . a good woman . . . a smart investigator—but still a flake. A cat-sitting flake who couldn't pick up a pair of kittens without constructing a wild criminal conspiracy.

Perhaps I had been too extreme in my kitten statement.

Had I said that Billy and Bob were the central players in the murders? I don't think so. If I said it, I really didn't mean it, and they should have known that.

But Billy and Bob had to be involved, involved in some important way. That's what I meant to convey. But my colleagues choked on that. And I became dispensable. Even old Sam Tully had abandoned me. Me, who had helped him resurrect Harry Bondo from the ashes. Me, whose investigative techniques were the model, Sam had claimed, for the new, kinder, gentler Harry Bondo. It was almost too much to bear.

I sat up abruptly, grabbed the address book from the table, and got Lila and Alex's home phone. I dialed. A recording informed me the number had been disconnected.

Which meant Asha had moved out.

I had no idea where she would go. But I had to find her. She would surely remember the name of the agency that had given Billy and Bob to Lila. It was essential that I get that information. And she knew about all the odd threats—or threatening oddities—Lila had received. She could tell me more about the party; at least everything she had told the police, and then some. She would help me, I knew that. She might have been a paid spy inserted into Alex and Lila's life by the Prospers, but the brutal deaths of Alex and Lila were not what she had bargained for.

Oh, yes. Contact with Asha was indispensable. The problem was, I realized, I did not know Asha's last name. Or where she would be. Or how to contact her through friends.

The homicide detectives would know, of course. I picked up the receiver to call them, then replaced it quickly. Was I really fool enough to believe they would tell me Asha's whereabouts? Right now, they probably wouldn't give me the phone number of the Police Athletic League.

A little agitation was beginning to join my depression.

Asha would have to wait. There were other people to contact. Other murky paths to explore.

Above all, it was time for me to speak to those people I had recognized at the party.

I lay back down and thought whom to contact first. Well, there was that musician, the one who had sent his regards to me through Greco and Fontana. And there was the baker. And the photographer. And . . .

A strange blankness seemed to overwhelm me. For

the life of me, I could not remember one name. Not one single name.

Enraged at my incompetence, I almost flung the phone.

But I didn't. I cooled down very quickly. I was starving. Maybe that was it. I hadn't had a bite of food since that chicken-salad sandwich in Room 601.

I walked into the kitchen and opened the refrigerator door. Pathetic. A few slices of stale bread in a wrapper. Some brown eggs. An onion and a half.

When I opened the bottom vegetable drawer, I found a small carton of hothouse cherry tomatoes I had purchased weeks ago. I had eaten only one of them. They were terrible.

The sight of them, though, excited me.

I would finally make a frittata. Like I had seen those two fat ladies make on television. Theirs had looked delicious.

I could, oddly enough, remember the recipe.

Sauté the cut-up tomatoes and sliced onions in a pan.

Then beat four eggs lightly. Beat. The dark-haired fat lady had been adamant that the eggs should not be whipped but beaten.

Then pour the sautéed onions and tomatoes into the eggs. Mix gently. Clean the pan with a paper towel. Pour the mixture back into the pan and cook slowly, on a very low fire. The fat lady had added fresh basil to her concoction, but that was pretty much out of the question for me.

Otherwise, no problem. Except I forgot what they had cooked the onions and tomatoes in. They were making an *Italian* omelet, they had emphasized. Not a French one. So it had to have been olive oil.

But I don't like olive oil in, around, or on my eggs. I like butter. After all, I grew up on a dairy farm in Minnesota.

But I had no butter. I had butter substitute—fake butter—so I used that, and began the first steps with a growing anticipation.

My, my, I was ravenous.

I watched greedily as the tomatoes and onions began to pop. The smell was delicious.

I broke the eggs and beat them carefully in a glass bowl. They waited.

I hovered over the pan.

The onions and tomatoes were ready. I poured them into the eggs, stirred slowly and thoroughly. Cleaned the pan with a paper towel and poured the fetal frittata back into the pan for its final journey.

I began to hum a bit and tap one foot on the floor.

Should I eat it right out of the pan when it was ready?

The frittata was cooking wonderfully, bubbling, rising and falling, struggling, solidifying.

I started to laugh. There was a new movie just out with Maggie Smith, called, I think, *Tea with Mussolini,* directed by Zeffirelli. I had always admired Maggie as an actress. Maybe there would be a sequel, called *Frittata with Mussolini*.

Maybe I would get the Maggie Smith role.

Such fantasies. It was almost ready. I slid the trusty spatula along the sides.

Then came the apparition. So suddenly and so unwilled and so brutal that I was literally swept out of reality.

There was a face in the frittata. And then a complete figure.

It was Hannah Prosper's.

She had a gun made of onions and tomatoes.

The murder played out in the pan, and this time it crushed me. Every part of me trembled. I winced as I heard the shots. I fell to my knees in unison with Timothy Prosper as he crashed down, his face and head a bloody mess.

And I screamed.

When I came to my senses, I don't know how much later, the frittata was all over the floor, my cats were hiding somewhere, and I was soaked with sweat.

It occurred to me that I had to get out of the apartment and talk to someone.

There was only Nora. She hadn't abandoned me.

Yes, I would go to Nora's place, and be among friends.

*   *   *

I crept into Nora's restaurant in the theater district—Pal Joey Bistro—at about eleven in the morning, an hour before it opened officially.

Nora kissed me and said Tony had called. He wanted to talk to me. About a misunderstanding. Then she didn't say another word. I must have looked pretty bad. She just led me to the table where her staff was being fed, and sat me down. That was fine with me. She flew off somewhere.

The staff lunch was served on the big rear table— large platters of salad, cold chicken breast, something that looked like chickpeas, sautéed string beans, and cookies.

There were seven people seated around the table besides me. Three young waitresses, two young men who delivered meals to the tables—"servers," I think they were called— and two older men, kitchen help. I think I had seen most of them at one time or another, but I didn't know their names.

As the platters were being passed to and fro, the others introduced themselves to me: Gwen, Ally, and Laura—the waitresses. Carey and Will—the servers. Hector and Porfino—the kitchen help.

I plucked two chicken breasts from the plate and began to devour them. Obviously, I would not have acted that precipitously had I not felt immediately at home.

I found this "at homeness" a bit disconcerting as I chewed. Where was I that I should have such comfort? Who were these people? The solution came quickly, even in my depressed, famished state.

Of course. I *was* at home. I was an out-of-work actress at a communal employee's table in a restaurant. I had worked for years as a waitress. Every actress I ever knew had done the same thing. I was like a hippo in a mud pool. I mean, for a hippo, no mud pool, however strange, is not soothing.

Not only were the place and the people welcoming—the chatter was familiar and endearing. I had heard it—oh, God—so many times. All about auditions, acting classes, agents, busted love affairs. Actors cannot be trusted, said the ladies. Actresses are bitches personified, said the men. On and on it went, and would go, as long as there was theater, theatergoers, restaurants to feed them, and out-of-work theater people to staff the restaurants.

The chicken was as tasty as the conversation. No frittata here. I felt much better after the second helping. I then settled for two huge cookies and a cup of coffee.

I could tell by the sidelong glances of two of the waitresses that they had now placed my face, professionally. Alice Nestleton—one of the hidden treasures of downtown theater, as a critic had called me. Chuckle, chuckle. But I was flattered.

I didn't like the cookies. I went for a little salad. I ate all I had put on my plate, and then I was satiated. The conversation, meanwhile, had become a bit grimmer and more focused. Still the den mother, I was silent and attentive. The server named Will was now speaking with urgency, and I realized with some embarrassment that he was talking about my friend Nora—his boss.

"She will never consider it . . . never!" he said. "She will never pay a dime toward medical benefits unless we frighten her. Unless we make it so uncomfortable . . ."

The waitress named Laura interrupted. "No restaurants pay benefits anymore."

"I know that. But it's changing back now. The Teamsters organized that new steakhouse uptown. They got good medical benefits. And believe it or not, vacation pay. Look, all I'm saying is, we meet with them. This place may be too small to organize anyway."

The waitress named Ally said wistfully: "Can you imagine what it would be like to have one of those IBM wrap-around policies? Dentists, shrinks, foot doctors, acupuncturists—Nirvana."

"Forget wrap-around," said Will. "Just basic hospitalization is a start. Hell, look what happened to Jerry. That could happen to any of us."

"What are you talking about?" the waitress Gwen asked. It was the first time I had heard her speak. She spoke in a low, guarded, almost tremulous voice. Very sexy. Very ingenue.

"You know! In and out of the hospital. Those bills

kept piling up. Sooner or later he had to get into bad hock. He had to get money from somewhere—anywhere."

"You don't know what you're talking about. It wasn't hospital bills that got Jerry into trouble. It was gambling," she retorted.

"Okay. Look, let's get back to the point. Let Jerry rest in peace. I miss that character. And I hope they get the creep who killed him. I hope they string him up."

It suddenly dawned on me that this Jerry they were talking about was none other than Jim Jerrard, the young man who had delivered my gift to Alex and Lila, and who had been murdered a few hours later by a loan shark.

And it was apparent that this young woman Gwen had been more than a coworker to him.

The table was cleared. I walked to the bar and chatted with Nora for a bit. She said I was looking much better. She wanted to ask about that bloodbath in Room 601, I knew, but she hesitated, and finally did not mention it. Nor did I encourage her. Patrons were beginning to arrive. She buzzed off and returned and was off again. The bar regulars filtered in.

I was feeling much better, my mind clear now. I was almost light-headed.

The conversation at the table had begun to interest me, retrospectively. Not the medical benefits aspect. Nor the way that Will the waiter—or server, or whatever he was—had couched his suggestions to meet with a Teamster representative in very soft and speculative terms—knowing, no doubt, that I was a friend of the owner.

No. It was his comments about the dead young man's repeated hospitalizations that intrigued me. It was most peculiar. But I didn't know why. After all, maybe Jerry just had chronic asthma or a bad back. I once had a boyfriend with such severe recurring lower back pain that his colleagues had to carry him into St. Vincent's emergency room on an average of twice a week to get muscle relaxer shots.

I did a strange thing then—a Sam Tully thing. I ordered a Brandy Alexander. I drank it very slowly, savoring it. I found myself becoming profoundly curious about that dead young man. Why? Again, I don't know. His was the only tragedy that had been all wrapped up. Sam and the police knew why and how and by whom he had been killed.

What difference did it make that he had often been hospitalized? So what?

I chided myself. Was this sudden morbid curiosity proof that I had as little faith in my kitten thesis as those who had abandoned me over it?

Nora stopped by again. Saw the drink in my hand. "Good idea," she said, and grinned indulgently.

I asked her: "Did you know that Jim Jerrard was in and out of hospitals?"

"I knew he missed work a lot," she replied.

"Because of hospitalization?" I pressed.

"Look, Alice, I'm in a labor dispute here. When you hear my staff talking, you have to take what they say with a grain of salt. How about a whole pillar of salt!"

I had pressed the wrong button. I changed the subject, or so Nora thought.

"Does that waitress Gwen work all day?" I asked.

"Only lunch today. She has an evening class."

"With whom?"

"Margie Black."

I had another drink. It would be a long afternoon. All acting classes from time immemorial always start at six in the evening.

I had the distinct and uncomfortable feeling that I was on a very old choo-choo train, chugging from one station to another in an attempt to find something relevant. This little station had kittens. And that little station had hospitalization. Who knew what the other stations had?

But it really didn't bother me in the least. Out-of-work actresses are like sharks. If they stop moving, they drown.

I believe now that I suffered a minor nervous breakdown during the murder of Timothy Prosper in Room 601.

That can be the only rational explanation for the sequence of events after the murder:

—the suppression of the memory of what really happened in 601 and other memory losses

—the emergence of my belief, without a shred of evidence to back it up, that the kittens Billy and Bob were at the center of the murders

—the . . . what shall I call it, an apparition? . . . the replay of the Room 601 horror in a stupid pan of eggs

—my obsessive fixation, so suddenly, on the many unexplained hospitalizations of a dead young man

—my coming up with all kinds of fanciful and inappropriate imagery in my thought and speech, such as sharks and choo-choo trains.

I walked to Fifth Avenue, found a Chase Bank, and cashed a check for $1,500—one half of what was left from my TV cop show gig.

Then I strolled to Burberry's on 57th Street and took about thirty seconds to purchase a long, dark-green winter coat with a huge collar for $948. I wore it out of the store after telling the sales clerk to give the coat I came in with to the thrift shop of her choice.

I then walked through Central Park in the freezing wind—heading north, heading toward that large, ugly building on 86th Street just off Central Park West. It was the building where Madame Black taught acting. I knew it. I had taken classes with her maybe ten or fifteen years ago. Not for long, of course.

I wasn't going there now to see her but to catch the waitress Gwen after class . . . to ask her . . . to demand of her that I be apprised of her dead lover's hospitalization history.

Is it not apparent that I was mentally disturbed at the time?

Why pursue the young waitress? What for? Why was that ridiculous information so sought after by me? For what bloody reason?

I didn't know. I think perhaps it was a belief which arose during the breakdown that my life had become allegorically a set of petty hospitalizations. An overblown way of looking at things, not really true. But I believe that was the cornerstone of my obsession.

Anyway, there was time to kill. So I spent several hours roaming the halls of the American Museum of Natural History. Searching out all the dioramas that contained the extinct beasts. When I found the sabertoothed tiger, I was ecstatic.

Gwen exited at seven-thirty onto the bleak, black, windswept street. She was a bit high, as good actresses always are after acting class.

I stepped in front of her, blocking her progress. Her eyes widened.

"Don't you remember me?"

"No."

"We ate lunch together about seven hours ago."

"Oh, yes. You. The boss's friend."

"I want to be Jerry's friend."

"Are you crazy? He's dead."

"Did you love him?"

"Of course, in my fashion."

"Why?"

"Because he was smart and crazy and funny. And everything he did got him deeper into trouble. And I thought maybe that love would—you know. What did it mean? Nothing. Anyway, now I've got to go!"

I didn't move. I didn't relent.

"Why was he hospitalized so many times?"

"Things always happened to him."

"Like what?"

"He'd walk in front of a car. He'd fall off a curb. He'd cut himself while peeling an apple. That's the way it was. Bad things always happened to him."

"Was he a drunk?"

"No."

"Suicidal?"

"Probably."

"Why couldn't he borrow the money to pay off his loans?"

"Didn't you ever see him perform?"

"No."

"If you had, you'd know why. He savaged everyone he knew. He thought it was a joke. They didn't. No one would do anything for him."

"Except you."

"Right. But I didn't have a dime. Believe me, he

tried to raise money. The poor fool did nothing but work. At Pal Joey and at the caterer's."

"What caterer?"

"In Chelsea. On Tenth and Twenty-sixth. The guy's name was Pat Ginko. Jerry made deliveries for him. All kinds of hours."

"I must've seen Jerry at Nora's. I know I did. But I don't remember what he looked like."

"And that's why you want to be his friend after he's dead?" She laughed at me in a brutal fashion.

"Did the police question you?"

"Again and again and again. They were crazy. They never stopped. They asked me about everything, from what kind of socks he wore to whether he liked sour cream and mushrooms."

"Were you working the night Jerry was shot?"

"No."

"Did he like cats?"

"What?"

"Cats!"

"No. He was allergic to them."

She was so young and so lovely and so indefinably odd. I had the sense that if I had a daughter, I would wish her to be like this girl. And I would understand when she fell in love with a borderline psychotic comic qua waiter qua gambler qua delivery boy with one foot always hovering over the grave.

The wind spun me around. I smiled.

"Please go. Thank you," I said.

She didn't leave just then. She pointed to the curb. "Do you see that curb? What is it . . . six inches high? Well, he would fall off it. Do you hear what I'm saying?" Then she walked away fast.

"Vertigo!" I shouted after her. "Perhaps he suffered from vertigo!"

Twenty minutes after my aggressive interview with Gwen, I was standing on the corner of 72nd Street and Columbus Avenue—perfectly healed.

I mean the breakdown had receded. The fissure had closed. I felt a bit tired, a bit cold, and a bit confused about the fuss I had been making.

Why I had pursued that girl up to her acting teacher's villa was incomprehensible to me now, only twenty minutes after I had interrogated her.

Likewise, my interest in dead Jerry and his hospitalizations. Why?

As for the new coat, I truly loved it, and I remembered purchasing it, but I could not for the life of me understand why I had spent almost a thousand dollars for it and got rid of a perfectly fine coat to boot.

I walked into the corner coffee shop, Timothy's, and ordered a cappuccino. This emotional blowout had come and gone so quickly, I began to wonder if one begins to suffer many little breakdowns as one grows older, like rashes. Perhaps they are so small and so innocuous that they are not recognized as such unless they show up as a face in a frittata.

As I sipped my cappuccino in the warm space, I began to suffer some rueful pangs. What an idiot I had been during the fissure.

I mean, I had truly believed that all my friends had abandoned me simply because they disagreed with me.

Had I acted on it? Had I insulted them? Abused them?

I couldn't remember. It was time, I thought, to repair what damage I might have done.

I went to the pay phone and called Tony. He wasn't home. Well, I knew where he was.

Then I called Sam Tully. He picked up at the first ring.

"Yeah?" he barked.

"Are you working, Sam?"

"Typing is not work, honey. It's like rough sex."

"Look, I want to apologize. I've been behaving badly lately, Sam."

"That's an understatement. Where are you?"

"Uptown."

"You got any money left?"

"Yes."

"Good. Don't apologize anymore. I want a hamburger. I want a big, expensive hamburger."

"Where?"

"What about that place on Spring Street . . . where

the beautiful people romp? Yeah, honey, I want to romp and eat."

"You mean Balthazar?" I asked. That was the place where A.G. Roth and I began our short-lived affair.

"Yeah, that's it. Eleven bucks for a hamburger. And they don't give you a pickle. I love it, honey. A half hour?"

"Fine."

There seemed to be hundreds of empty cabs uptown. Maybe it was the weather. People didn't want to brave the winter winds unless they had to.

Sam was waiting outside the restaurant when I arrived. He looked like he was freezing.

"Why didn't you go on in?"

"Manners," he said. "A lady of your quality should not have to enter a pub alone."

"This isn't a pub, Tully. It's Balthazar."

We walked in and sat at a booth near the long, elegant bar.

The waiter approached.

Sam asked me: "Are you sure you got the bread?"

I smiled, touched the fabric of my thousand dollar new coat, which he hadn't even noticed, and said, "I am flush."

"Good. I'm hungry and thirsty."

He ordered a brandy and coffee, a rare burger, and a crabcake appetizer.

I ordered a brandy with soda on the side and the crabcakes. No hamburger.

The waiter left. Sam sat back, lit a cigarette, and grinned: "So you been around the bend, huh, Nestleton?"

"I'm quite sure of it," I said, and then told him the tale of my life since I left the wake thinking my comrades had abandoned me. The story culminated in my obsessive assault on Gwen for information on her dead lover.

The drinks arrived. My story continued. The crab-cakes arrived—and by then I was through.

I picked at my food. He downed his brandy as if it were cheap bourbon and ordered another one. Then he pronounced judgment: "That was one hell of a story, honey."

"Don't you believe it?"

"Of course I do. What I don't get is why you fastened on that dead kid. I mean, when you started babbling about those kittens—well, at least they were the dead lady's cats."

"Do you want me to be philosophical, Sam?"

"That is my *métier*."

I laughed at the lovable old fool's affectation.

"Well, we all know people who hurt themselves physically. Ostensibly, they're just accident prone. Right? Now, I've never suffered from accident-proneness, you understand. Not in a physical sense, that is. But in the sense of life choices, I always have. With men, with apartments, with parts, with acting teachers. I always did the same thing intellectually that poor Jim Jerrard seemed to have done physically. And like him, I always gambled, and I always lost."

Sam found that darkly humorous: "But, honey, no loan shark ever put a slug in your head."

"That's true, Sam."

"So drink to your escape," he said.

I did. The hamburger came. He ate it slowly, with a kind of speculative intensity.

Halfway through, he stopped eating, pulled my hand across the table, and kissed it gallantly, saying, "I shall always be indebted to you, baby, for providing me with those unique sensations of loathing and exhilaration which can only come from eating a small, mediocre hamburger that costs eleven dollars."

I leaned back, smiling, and closed my eyes. I would have to apologize to all my friends. It might, I realized, turn out to be an expensive undertaking.

I drank more brandy. I was beginning to get that buzz.

"You should get bombed, honey," Sam said. "Sobriety at this stage is contraindicated."

I thought of the young actress Gwen and the way she had looked when she walked out of her acting class. So anticipatory. Yes! That was it! I wondered whether she would make it.

"What kind of affair do you think it was, Sam?"

"What are you talking about?"

"I mean the love between that young woman and the dead comedian."

"No different from any other, probably."

"No, no. It had to be different. More intense maybe."

"Why?"

"Because comics are always intense and crazy. I mean, there seems to be a tradition of that. Bruce. Belushi. Kaufman. Pryor. Right? Drugs, booze, jail—lunacy of all kinds. To tell you the truth, I never understood that. I mean, comics are usually smarter and more compassionate than most people. That's what their routines are all about. At least the modern ones. They uncover hypocrisy and they mock it. That's rational."

"A lot of not-funny people are self-destructive also, honey."

"Maybe."

"Look at me."

"What about you?"

"When I was young, honey, I would fall off curbs also. And worse. I remember once I took a job writing pornographic novels. Me, I had never read that junk and I didn't know how to write it. But I needed cash real bad. I mean to tell you, I couldn't afford a roll and butter. So I took the assignment and promised delivery in thirty days. Like I said, I didn't know what I was doing. So I went to see some dirty movies on 42nd Street. Then I sat down and wrote the damn book. I mailed it off. And waited for my five-hundred-dollar check. Now, as I'm waiting I'm walking a lot—hungry. One night, I'm looking in shoe store windows 'cause I needed a new pair when that check came. I see something real nice and comfortable looking. I lean forward. But I misjudge the space and wallop my face into the glass. Damn thing takes about twenty stitches to close. Look!"

He leaned toward me and spread one eyebrow. The scar was still clearly visible.

"But Sam," I said, "you're an . . ."

I stopped suddenly, embarrassed at what I was going to say.

"But, honey, I wasn't an alkie until I was forty."

"You mean you were clean and sober then?"

He found that so funny, he almost fell out of the booth.

"Sober? Yes. Clean? Hell, no. I was a hack writer. You know who's the patron saint of hack writers, don't you?"

"I haven't the slightest idea."

"Saint Dustin the Green."

"Who was he?"

Another bout of uproarious laughter. He removed his stubby horse player's pencil from his pocket, signaled secrecy with a finger to his lips, then wrote in large letters on the napkin:

DEXAMYL

Then something very strange happened. We were both staring at the word. Then we both fell off the curb. But we both clambered up again. I was shaken by it. Tully just looked profoundly sad. He spoke softly: "One of us, honey, is a bloody genius at what used to be called the art of criminal investigation."

We left fast. We had to move fast. There was someone to see.

The name of the establishment on the corner of 26th Street and Tenth Avenue was Very Chelsea.

It was one of the new-type catering places that were springing up in diverse parts of the city—a kind of testament to the fact that there were now a great many affluent people about, no matter the neighborhood.

They catered any and all kinds of affairs; the hipper and more discriminating the food preferences, the better. And they also functioned as restaurants and coffee shops. People walked in off the street, went to the counter, ordered what they wanted from the large menu, and ate it right there, on simple butcher-block tables.

Very Chelsea wrapped around the corner, with its main entrance on 26th Street. Sam and I arrived a little before 10 P.M. The door was locked.

But there was obviously some sort of activity going on in the back of the place. The large kitchen was flooded with light.

We peered in through the spotlessly clean windows.

A man and a woman stood conversing. The man was wearing a chef's outfit. The woman, quite young, in street clothes, held a pad and pencil in her hand.

The kitchen was definitely closed. All around the room, gleaming pots were piled neatly. One wall contained an enormous stock of diverse containers, every size and shape, used to pack food for delivery.

It dawned on me that I had no idea how Pal Joey Bistro had delivered the meal I had sent to Lila and Alex. I mean—what kind of container? Maybe the food had not gone out in a container—just a platter covered with clear plastic.

"Is that Pat Ginko?" Sam asked, indicating the chef.

"It has to be."

"Who's the girl?"

"I don't know. I don't know anything about the place or this Ginko, except that Jerrard worked for him."

"He's a new face," Sam said.

I understood what he was thinking: that no one knew about this Ginko before, not us, not the NYPD, not anyone who was looking for information. This fact . . . along with our mutual revelation that persistent falling off of curbs is often indicative that one is introducing an alien substance into one's body, maybe even little green pills, tiny, beautifully formed and clefted emeralds of paradise, and these tiny items elicit brave acts, unmediated by fear or confusion; in other words, you fall and you laugh, you leap and you laugh . . . so it was that revelation, and as I said, the fact that Ginko was an unknown element, which glued us like children to the glass pane.

The young woman headed out of the kitchen toward the door. Sam and I moved to an adjoining building. Bent over against the cold wind—and believe me, the wind blows in Chelsea in winter with a nonurban ferocity—she was not aware of us at all, although she passed only an arm's length away.

We returned to our surveillance point.

Sam whispered to me urgently: "Don't you feel it, honey? This character knows something."

I nodded in affirmation, though to be quite honest, since I had recovered from my fissure, or nervous breakdown, call it what you will, I had become hyperrational and skeptical.

"Let's grab him when he comes out," Sam suggested.

Ginko, if it was he, didn't emerge. He leaned against a counter and lit a cigarette, looking rather rakish in his chef's hat.

He seemed to be slipping deeper and deeper into a kind of post-cooking reverie, which I always assumed bears some analogy to postcoital reverie. This of course I did not mention to Sam.

We watched, numb from the cold.

"How old does he look to you?" Sam asked.

"Forty, maybe."

"He's skinny. At least six foot three," Sam noted. "He looks like a Finn. I mean, what I think a Finn should look like."

We waited and watched.

"Do you get the feeling we're in a Hopper painting? The deserted city. Night. A lit coffee shop. A single, anonymous man inside."

"You're right, Sam. It's eerily Hopperish."

"You know, there's a guy in Chicago, a professor, who wrote a book about film noir, and he says the real heavy influence on those directors and cameramen who made those films were not writers, but painters. And particularly Hopper. How does that grab you?"

"People from Chicago are interesting but strange," I replied.

We were not able to explore the topic further. From inside there came a dim, muffled sound. The telephone was ringing. We saw Ginko walk to the wall phone and pick it up. He seemed to be listening, not talking. He hung up the phone.

All at once he was running out of the kitchen—through the fire exit that opened onto Tenth Avenue.

We didn't have time to react to his movement, let alone stop him.

He began to trot down the avenue, off the sidewalk, near the curb.

"What the hell is going on with this guy?" Sam gasped as we struggled to keep the cook in sight.

Ginko stopped suddenly on the corner of Twenty-second and Tenth Avenue. He looked around. Then he walked slowly west, onto the block with all the new art galleries. They were shut down for the night already.

He headed for a large, ugly old panel truck parked halfway to Eleventh.

We crossed to the other side. Ginko vanished into the truck.

We waited again. He was in there about five minutes. When he came out, he had a small carry-all with a shoulder strap.

The truck drove off, right past us.

I stared in disbelief.

Ginko started to walk slowly back toward Tenth Avenue.

"Now! Let's stop him now!" Sam urged.

"No," I said quietly.

"What do you mean, no? We have to get some answers."

"No," I repeated quickly, "we'll keep following him."

"But why?"

"Because the truck that just passed us had a sign on it. NOZAK FOR FINE BAKED GOODS, it said. And Nozak was at the party."

Sam stopped arguing the point. Ginko walked south on Tenth Avenue until 14th Street; then east on 14th Street to Sixth Avenue; then south on Sixth Avenue.

Now he was walking slowly, leisurely. At Bleecker Street, he crossed to the east side of Sixth Avenue. Then he stopped for the light at Houston Street. We were about twenty yards back. The light turned green. He crossed. We hurried to make the light also.

He kept heading south. We passed a grim little park on the left, where the homeless bed down in all sorts of weather. Sam and I stared in. We saw wrapped bodies lying on top of benches.

Suddenly Ginko was no longer in sight. It was as if Sixth Avenue had swallowed him up.

"He went into the park," Sam said.

Yes. That had to be it. We rushed through the small entrance. There were no people on their feet. Just all those sleeping figures like so many dirty mummies. I panicked and started to pull Sam out.

Then we saw them. Two people standing close together at the wall that enclosed the south end of the little park.

They saw us, too. Ginko burst forward and punched Sam in the chest. Poor Tully went down.

Ginko ran. The other figure ran in the opposite direction, toward the Houston Street exit. I saw the carry-all bag he carried, and grabbed at it.

The figure screamed and pulled.

Still on the ground, Sam was yelling, "Get him! Get him!"

My hands, entwined in the strap, jerked again and again. I was being pulled along.

The figure tripped over a sleeping man wrapped in black trash bags—and fell hard to the ground, taking me along. I fell on my knees, bruised and hurting.

But my protagonist was hurting too. We were face-to-face. Sam crawled up, cursing, and zipped open the bag. He reached inside and pulled out a clear plastic sandwich baggie. He held it up high to catch the moonlight.

Inside the baggie was what seemed to be a sheaf of fifty-dollar bills—like carefully stacked slices of baloney.

I couldn't have cared less. I was interested in the figure breathing heavily on the ground beside me.

A small, slight figure dressed in boys' clothes.

It was no boy, though. It was, beyond a doubt, Cynthia Quarles, the manager of the Red Witch.

Chapter 14

Three silent, wounded people sat at a table in the Red Witch. It was one in the morning. We were waiting for Greco and Fontana. They were waiting for a search warrant.

Cynthia Quarles had not said a single word since the encounter in the park. She had in fact slipped into a zombielike state; not trying to get away; not listening; not reacting to light or sound or cold.

Sam and I had taken her into a bar on Varick Street. There we had treated our wounds. Sam had a little trouble breathing. My knees were bloody.

I called the NYPD. Greco called back sleepily in thirty minutes. I described the contents of the bag—packets upon packets of fifties. He ordered us to get over to the Red Witch as soon as possible and wait for him.

Well, we took an hour or so to recover and then proceeded to West 3rd Street.

Cynthia did not withhold the keys.

At twenty minutes to two, Detectives Greco and Fontana, the search warrant, and four uniformed officers arrived.

Sam and I gave our statements.

Cynthia Quarles refused to open her mouth. She now seemed less zombielike, though, less in shock. She kept looking at me and Sam like an animal in a trap. Seeking help from strangers. Didn't she understand that we wouldn't help her? We had put her into the trap.

The searchers started to take the restaurant apart.

Sam whispered, "For some reason, honey, this always relaxes me."

I could see that Cynthia was now watching the searchers. She seemed to have gotten smaller and smaller—like a tiny bird.

Fontana kept coming over to us, circling us, making rather pointed quips, incomprehensible ones, about how even broken clocks are right twice a day. He was very unhappy with Sam and me. But also anticipatory.

To make a long story short, the searchers found what they were looking for in less than an hour—in the bricks lining the dumbwaiter that brought the food up from the kitchen and took the dirty dishes down.

They found a great deal of money—fifty-dollar bills in packets.

And they found a bewildering array of amphetamines—pills, crystals, liquid vials.

All of it was then heaped onto the table, next to where the three of us sat.

Greco stuck his face close to Cynthia's: "You don't have any option anymore. You understand? It's all here. You killed that old couple, didn't you? And who else? What about the kid? The waiter. You kill him also? Who was the guy you met in the park?"

He shot a dozen or so more questions at her, tapping the evidence on the adjoining table.

Then Fontana said: "What I can't understand is, are you *making* this money? Are you laundering the money? Are you pushing the stuff? Are you warehousing the stuff? Who are you, Miss Quarles? There's enough on that table to put you away for five-hundred years of federal time."

Greco came back with a footnote: "Talk to us. We don't care about the stuff. We're not DEA. We're NYPD Homicide detectives. Talk to us. We're the only friends you've got."

Phoebe, the restaurant cat, appeared out of nowhere and clambered up on Cynthia's lap. Phoebe was large, fat, and silent. Cynthia pushed her down gently. The cat sauntered off to inspect the tumult in the dumbwaiter. Then Cynthia began to talk in the low but very persuasive tone that was her maitre d' trademark. She was speaking for the record, but she was speaking to me. She was looking at Greco and Fontana, but in a weird way she was turned toward me.

"I am afraid that you have no understanding at all of what happened. It is not something that happened right now. It goes back a long time. Alex and Lila were my parents, my grandparents, my mentors, my focus, my life. They were the kindest, finest people I have ever met or ever will meet. They lived for others. They didn't give a damn about their situation, financial or otherwise. They gave shelter to others when they didn't have the rent for themselves. They started this silly restaurant primarily to feed indigent actors. Believe me, that's what this restaurant is all about.

"The story is very simple. They hired me to make the Red Witch a success. That was impossible. It should have been closed ten years ago. They refused to close it. They believed I would find a way. What was I, a magician? I could pull the overhead out of a hat?"

"A baker gave me a way. Nozak. He was a fine baker. But he makes his money distributing amphetamines. You know who most of his customers are? Fine chefs in fine Manhattan restaurants. Because it seems that when a busy chef has to prepare a hundred dinners in two hours—it's the only drug that works. It makes his head clear; it gives him enormous powers of memory. It makes him fast and accurate. It makes him Super Chef.

"Nozak said all I had to do was store the stuff and the money, and he would give me enough to keep the Red Witch alive. Four thousand dollars a month. My accountant kept asking me how the restaurant stayed afloat. I finally told him that I was putting cash into the business. He told me to report it as a loan and deduct the interest. I didn't, of course. He didn't press me. He just said that as long as I reported receipts accurately and didn't play around with the withholding taxes, there would be no problem. Federal, state, and local tax people, he said, don't care how much money you put into a business, only how much you take out without giving them their cut.

"There was one other thing I had to do. Provide temporary employment to chefs who were out of work and wanted to earn money. They worked here a few months, distributed the speed throughout the city, and then took off. They liked it that way. Nozak liked it that way. Everybody in and out fast. Nozak had no permanent employees except me and Ginko.

"Now, Ginko needed an assistant from time to time. He picked the wrong one. A speed freak named Jerrard. A comedian. He was in financial trouble. He stole speed from us. Ginko cut him off . . . fired him. Jerrard begged me to intercede. I couldn't. He begged me to talk to Alex and Lila. I told him the old people didn't even know the operation existed. He didn't believe me. He told me Alex and Lila were strangling him to death.

"Dear Alice Nestleton provided the spark. Of course, she could not know that a waiter at the place where she ordered her gift had means and motive to kill the people the gift was meant for.

"It happened. They died miserably. It was not hard for me to figure out who had done it. I called Nozak. I told him I was through unless he brought me the soul of that waiter in a box—or his head. I was crazy, believe me. It must have been Nozak who killed Jerrard. And in my way, I rejoiced. But Alex and Lila were gone. Everything was gone. I gave Nozak notice anyway. The meeting with Ginko in the park was to be my last."

She placed her head down on the table.

Greco bent over and stared into her face. "You're double-talking."

"I told you the truth."

"Let's go over one fact again. It's unclear. Did you order Nozak to kill the waiter?"

"No. I couldn't order Nozak to do anything. I worked for him. Maybe I wished for Jerrard's death. Maybe I asked for his death. Maybe I tried to blackmail Nozak into killing him. But I never said those words—'Kill him.' I told you the truth. I threatened. I babbled. I talked all kinds of nonsense about him bringing me the head and soul of Jerrard. But anyone would be a fool to take me literally. I believe now I did not truly wish it."

"Do you use amphetamines?"

"No."

"How was it possible to keep that old couple from knowing what was going on in their own restaurant?"

"Suspicion of any kind was not in their makeup."

Fontana laughed and took over the questioning. "Are you telling us that all four thousand dollars a month you got from Nozak in storage fees went to the restaurant?"

"I took two hundred a week to live on. The rest went to the Red Witch. From time to time I saved on food costs and gave the cash to Alex and Lila."

The questioning went on and on. I dozed off. There was nothing more I really wanted to hear. There was nothing I had to say.

It was almost five in the morning when the Red Witch cleared out. They took Cynthia Quarles away. They left the mess and Phoebe.

Sam was still there, though. He had smoked up all his cigarettes. He was exhausted and grumpy. He started circling the dining room, kicking at the legs of chairs.

I looked up, bemused: "Not enough excitement for the night?" I asked.

"I got a lousy taste in my mouth, honey. I can't even congratulate you. I mean, you do deserve some kind of award for fixing on a totally meaningless fact while having a nervous breakdown—a fact that turned out to be the break in the case. But I think I'll let Payne Whitney give you the reward. You see, honey, what I can't get out of my mind is that your friends Alex and Lila are dead because of mistaken identity. They were not involved in the amphetamine business. It doesn't stop there, does it? I mean, Hannah Prosper thought they were involved in and orchestrated her baby-sitter's betrayal. Right? But you heard what Cynthia Quarles said. They were goddamn saints—angels. Don't you echo that opinion? Didn't you think they were a breed apart . . . a couple apart . . . the Saint Francis and Saint Teresa of the theater world and the restaurant world and even the damn kitty adoption world? Do you see where I'm going with this, honey? Do you see the kind of philosophical problems that are going to emerge in my everyday existence?"

It was a very stupid speech.

He didn't know what he was saying. And I didn't know what he was saying. Luckily for all, he sat down, or seemed to collapse.

I realized that I had not removed my one-thousand-dollar Burberry coat since I had purchased it. I also realized I had no idea who Cynthia Quarles was, or whether she had told the truth. And if she had, why did I feel the truth to be tinny, anticlimactic, banal, soap-operaish? Where was the gargoyle?

Sam muttered something.

"What?"

"One more problem, honey."

He pointed at Phoebe, who was perched on the lip of the dumbwaiter.

In response, I pointed at one of the movie posters on the wall. He pointed at a pepper shaker. I pointed at the hem of my new coat. He pointed at his left ear.

We both burst out laughing at our pathetic pointing game, the silly game we had suddenly invented, the name and rules to be disclosed some time in the future.

As one of the heroes of the newly emerging psychoanalytic movement in Vienna in the 1920s once said—was it Ferenzi?—"Detection deranges one." His patient had been an Austrian police inspector with a strong desire to dress as a woman, and a stronger fear that he would do so on the job.

Chapter 15

Believe me, compared to Minnesota winters, New York winters are balmy. Except for the wind. There is something about the wind in New York City that is incredibly raucous. Maybe because there are so many buildings for it to bounce off. Anyway, I had recovered quite nicely except for a small, recurring, edgy depression that I attributed to windswept days one after another.

Ten days after the apprehension of Cynthia Quarles, A.G. Roth invited me to his apartment, saying that he had a most spectacular gift for me in tribute to my investigative brilliance.

When I entered the apartment, Billy and Bob were fast asleep on the rug, crazily entangled as kittens often are, though it was obvious to the discerning eye that they were very quickly moving away from kittenhood.

A.G. was dressed quite well—for him. I sat down and he handed me a very large, flat, gift-wrapped package. I placed it on my knees.

"Well, open it," he said.

"Don't rush me. I just arrived."

He went into the kitchen and brought me back a cup of espresso, the product of a newly acquired espresso machine, which I had advised against, since the man was totally incompetent in matters electronic and electrical.

"So, either drink the espresso or open the package," A.G. demanded.

I put the espresso down and opened the package.

It was ghastly. The fool had gotten me, probably at an exorbitant price, a twenty-year-old calendar featuring on each page brilliant closeup photos of the gargoyles on the Church of Notre Dame in Paris.

I didn't say a word. He looked confused. He said: "I am beginning to get the feeling that this was an inappropriate gift."

"Are you?"

He walked to the other side of the room and sat down, placing his head in his hands as if he had a headache. "In fact, I am beginning to realize that there is something peculiar about our relationship, and this peculiarity mainly lies in the fact that you continually force me to act inappropriately."

"Ah. Then I forced you to buy me this gift?"

"Wait. Not overtly. What I'm saying is, this is a

subliminal thing. And what happened between us was that this subliminal hostility negated the sublimeness of our relationship."

"Oh, my God, A.G. Do you have any idea how stupid you sound?"

"Then you tell me why we are no longer lovers."

"Like my friend Mr. Tully says in his inimitable New York style, it's for me to know and for you to find out."

"I shall change the subject."

"Good idea."

"If you don't want the gift, I'll give it to someone else."

"No, no . . . no, no. I'll take it. Thank you very much. Everyone knows I have a thing with gargoyles."

"Believe me, Alice, it was not meant to open the Baby Kate sore."

"I have no 'sore,' as you put it, concerning the Baby Kate case. I . . . we . . . all of us . . . for whatever reason we were in it . . . did our best. And the fact of the matter is, we changed nothing."

"Come on, Alice. We got Timothy Prosper blown away."

"Don't make me say 'If ever a man deserved it . . .' Because I'm not. I wish he still lived."

His voice lowered considerably. He said: "You know, I think about Baby Kate a lot. I have the feeling that the child is okay. That the baby-sitter took the ransom money, took the child, and is now living some kind of bucolic existence in the Southwest. Maybe San Antonio. Maybe Santa Fe. But I have this feeling it's in the Southwest. Dry, hot air. And they ride horses on weekends and they wear red bandannas."

I didn't say a word. Yes, of course I had been thinking about Baby Kate. But I did not share A.G.'s optimism. Not at all.

The phone rang once, twice, three times. A.G. answered it. There was a brief, barking conversation. The last words I heard him say before he hung up were: "I hope you got it straight this time. Just deliver what you're supposed to deliver."

I had a sinking feeling in my stomach.

"A.G., what was that conversation about?"

"Nothing important."

"I really hope you are not ordering in any food."

He started to laugh, rollicking peals of laughter, so hearty he woke the kittens and off they ran. When he composed himself, he whispered: "You may find me untrustworthy, Miss Nestleton, but you know there will be no sour cream."

"I don't want any pizza, I don't want any sandwiches, I don't want any danish pastries. About the only thing I feel like right now is an aspirin, and you don't have to have that delivered."

"Why don't you wait till it arrives?"

"Sure."

"I want to talk to you about something else before we eat."

"Go right ahead."

"I think Cynthia Quarles is going to get off with an exceedingly light term."

"You may be right."

"Alas, I also think that with good lawyers Mrs. Prosper can end up serving less than five years."

"How do you figure that?"

"She doesn't contest the murder of her husband. The man gave her a venereal disease while she was pregnant. No jury on earth would give her more than five years given the circumstances. And I believe she will retract her confession on the kidnapping. I believe there is not enough evidence to prove that she set up a fake kidnapping which turned into a real one. I believe the only witness with any credibility whatsoever is that girl Asha. The problem is, we don't know how much Asha knew. They paid her to spy on the old couple. I think all she knew was that the Prospers believed the old couple knew the kidnapper. That's all. Do you know what I'm saying, Alice?"

"This is speculation."

"Of course, of course. I know it's speculation."

"It's as speculative as a Southwestern venue for the vanished pair."

"You have a point."

"Good. Now, A.G., why don't you sit back in your chair and relax and talk to me like I was your shrink or your acting coach. Why did you get me this ridiculous calendar?"

He was silent for a long time. He fiddled with his feet, crossing them and uncrossing them, staring at the tips of his shoes. A.G. usually wore horrendous shoes, but this evening he was wearing a pair of highly buffed oxfords. Like a country gentleman.

He raised his finger in the air: "If you want the truth and nothing but the truth, Alice, I think I did it simply as a memento. You know. We had made love, and we had done a whole lot of things together. But this was the first time I really worked intensely with you. And with your friends. And it was something I treasured. I don't think you treasured my participation that much. But I think you know in your heart you were very brave and very smart. You were the Cat Woman. So I gave you a bloody memento."

"That's sweet, A.G."

The doorbell rang.

Please read on for an excerpt from the next Alice Nestleton mystery. Coming from Signet in Summer 2002.

How hot was that August night? So hot that even with both loft ceiling fans going at high speed and all my large windows wide open I had to abandon my bed and seek cooler space on the floor, using a terry cloth towel as a sleeping mat.

I was, by then, totally naked. And this, for some reason, unnerved Pancho a bit; he ceased his all-weather pursuit of nonexistent enemies. In fact, my stubby-tailed, dim-witted gray cat just stared at me as if I were a total stranger. Bushy, my Maine coon cat, would have been more sophisticated. But he was staying overnight at the vet, getting his nails done, his health examined, and his attitude adjusted.

It had been so far a slow, constricting, jobless, loveless summer. And it was not over yet. Most of my friends had vanished. Nora was once again taking her vacation on Martha's Vineyard. Tony Basillio was in Los Angeles, looking, he said, for work. Chuckle, chuckle. A.G. Roth, believe it or not, had gone to England for his long-awaited opportunity to make, as he put it, on-the-scene, hard-hitting inquiries concerning the British Secret Service's role in the assassination of Abraham Lincoln. His obsession with this case seemed not only to be ballooning, but now was a full-blown psychosis that in my opinion required hospitalization. I have heard that lawyers are particularly prone to this sort of thing.

The only one of my "circle" not away from the city was Sam Tully, but he was incommunicado unless you met him in a bar. And that I refused to do in the summer. In hot weather any type of alcohol makes me sick. I can't even stand to be around the stuff. Of course in fall and winter, and even spring, I'm a bit more tolerant.

I had been reading a lot, particularly Henry James. I had always disliked his novels and could never finish a single one. But I had recently found at the Strand a collection of his tales, and they were mesmerizing. Perhaps it was the heat. Anyway, while waiting or looking for jobs, either cat related or theater related, I would read him in spurts.

So that is the way my summer was going—a little of this and a little of that.

That is, until the phone call on that hot night while I was lying nude on the floor.

Usually, when one is naked on the floor at eleven

o'clock on a very hot and sultry summer evening, one expects some kind of romantic thing.

The voice, however, was very prosaic. So was our conversation.

"Is this Alice Nestleton?"

"Yes. Who is this?"

"You don't know me. My name is Louis Montag. I need a cat-sitter and you were recommended to me."

"By whom?"

"By a man in a bar. I think his name was Samuel."

Uh-oh, I thought. If this Montag was drinking in the same bar that Sam was, it had to be a seedy, ugly bar. Did I really want to have a business arrangement with him? Any kind of arrangement? But he did sound rather normal.

He waited for me to say something. I didn't say anything. So he went on.

"Here's the deal. I need a cat-sitter a couple of nights a week. Maybe three. A few hours each of those nights, maybe between eight and midnight. The cat's name is Brat. He's not a problem, except he keeps bothering me when I'm working on my laptop. I'm a writer. He seems to be infatuated with the laptop screen. When I lock him in another room, he starts screeching. So that's what I need a cat-sitter for. You get it? I'll be at my laptop making a living, and Brat will be entertained by you, hopefully, in another room."

"Where is your place?"

"I have a loft on the Bowery. Just south of Houston. I thought ten dollars an hour would be fair. And an extra ten for the cab home. That would come to fifty dollars for the evening. Is that acceptable to you, Miss Nestleton?"

Usually, I wouldn't consider it immediately acceptable. Just on general principle. But times were bad. "Are you air-conditioned, Mr. Montag?"

"To the hilt."

"We have a deal."

"Good. Tomorrow night?"

"Fine."

"By the way, I never used a cat-sitter before. Am I supposed to provide food for you?"

I laughed. "No, not really. A piece of fruit would be nice, though. And something cold to drink."

He gave me the address and said that I should not worry at all about Brat—except for his laptop fetish, he was a delightful creature. Of course I had heard such claims before.

And that was that with the phone call.

I tried to go to sleep. It was a bit difficult. I read some James, but my eyes hurt in the heat.

At a little past midnight, I heard the blessed sound of thunder approaching. Louder and louder. I switched off the ceiling fans. The storm hit. Sudden and furious. The heavens opened. Wind and water whipped through my large windows.

As quickly as the storm came, it left. And in its wake was silence and cool.

I drifted off into sleep.

Some time close to dawn, I woke with an itch on my left leg. At least at first I thought it was an itch. But then I realized it was a bug crawling from my knee down toward my toe.

I sat up and leaned forward to swat the intruder.

Then I saw to my horror that it was a baby mouse crawling down my leg. I mean a very tiny and very young baby mouse.

Now, intellectually, I love and admire all God's creatures. Rodents included.

But in the real world I had become deathly afraid of them, like the stereotype dizzy blonde who screams and climbs up on a chair at the sight of a mouse. It happened very suddenly, about two years ago. I don't know why. Maybe some complex reaction to aging. What was really interesting about my newly formed mouse fear was that it only became severe when I was alone or lonely or feeling abandoned by humans.

Anyway, I gave out one of those stereotypical squeaks of horror . . . half moan, half scream, all embarrassing. It would be hard for anyone hearing such a performance to know that the performer, as a girl, had calmly eaten breakfast every morning in a Minnesota farmhouse with clearly visible field mice chattering on a nearby kitchen shelf, looking for sugar.

The baby mouse dashed off me; obviously it now realized I was not its mother. It scooted under the dining room table where it just stopped and waited by one of the legs.

Crouched on the floor about five feet away from the baby mouse was old Pancho.

He was crouched real low, like a leopard in the grass. And if he still had a tail, no doubt it would have been twitching, for his eyes were focused on the prey under the table.

Brave, noble, modest Pancho. He would protect my home and hearth. I winced, realizing I was about to witness the central ritual of the wild—a kill.

The baby mouse realized his or her situation. It remained absolutely still under the gaze of that ferocious stalker Pancho.

Then the baby mouse made his move. Toward the closet, where there were enough holes around the perimeter to move a regiment of full-grown mice.

Now, I thought. It's going to happen now. I braced myself for the carnage.

Pancho didn't move. He just sat there and watched the little mouse disappear. I felt a sudden rage. I screamed at him: "You coward! You traitor! Why didn't you protect me? Why didn't you *do* something?"

When I realized how ridiculous I was being, I just

sank back down onto the Turkish towel and watched the morning light emerge, on the verge of tears, but never getting there.

The next morning I retrieved Bushy from the vet and told him the whole shameful story, saying that his partner Pancho had exhibited extreme cowardice in the line of duty. Bushy did not appear to be surprised.

In the afternoon I went to the Film Forum and saw a 1970s comedy, *Welcome to Greenwich Village*. Then I went to an air-conditioned Starbuck's on Spring Street and read Henry James on and off while eating a chocolate chip muffin and drinking two iced coffees. (The refill was half price.)

At seven-thirty I walked the six or seven blocks to the Bowery and rang the downstairs industrial-type bell of Louis Montag's dwelling.

I was buzzed in. I walked up a wide set of concrete stairs to the third landing. Montag was waiting for me at the open door.

"Did you have any trouble finding me?" he asked.

"Not at all," I replied.

He opened the door wide, allowing me to enter. I was struck immediately by his height—he towered over me—and his crookedness. His shoulders were extremely uneven and stooped, and his elbows looked as if they had been broken and reset. He was dark complexioned with longish hair for a man his age—he seemed about forty-five—and he was dressed like a Soho painter, in sandals without socks, a ripped tee shirt, and carpenter jeans of great age and disrepair.

He didn't look at me when he spoke; his eyes seemed fixed about an inch to the right of my face.

The loft was quite nice; sparsely furnished, freshly painted, and heavily air-conditioned.

It was divided in two by a single set of sliding doors. One entered into the work area. From where I stood I could see the sleeping area through the doors. That was where, I supposed, I would be entertaining the cat. It looked large and comfortable.

In the work area, where I was standing, there were two long tables meeting each other at the corners. On them were two desk computers and a laptop, along with a printer, a fax machine, and a bewildering array of phone equipment which spilled over onto the floor.

One wall was essentially a book case.

And one wall had a hodgepodge collection of blown-up book covers, hung with abandon—in no particular pattern. Some were framed and others were not.

They were obviously the covers for different editions of the same book. And when I got close enough to read the title—*New York by Night*—I realized why the name Montag had resonated in my head with a gentle tickle.

Montag and Fields were the authors of this rather famous guidebook to the New York cultural underworld, if one could call it that.

"Would you like a drink, Miss Nestleton?" he asked. I liked his formality. He asked the question almost with a bow. And he had one of those pleasant New York accents—soft and gruff at the same time.

I could see the tray he had set up on the sink counter in the small kitchen. These lofts all had tiny, open wall kitchens, put in when the spaces were converted from industrial use.

"Not right now."

"Well, please sit down," he suggested.

There were several chairs in the work area. But they all seemed to be knockoffs of the old elementary school chairs, with large folding arms. I smiled at the lack of options and sat down. "I'd like to see Brat now."

He replied: "I'm afraid he's not here right now."

"What?"

"Oh, there's nothing to worry about. He'll be here in a short while. The walker has him."

"You have a cat walker?" I asked incredulously.

"Yes. Brat needs to get out. He's hyperactive. Someone usually walks him from about four to six. Today the walker was a bit late."

"On a leash?" I asked. I was starting to get a bit suspicious. Was this man just eccentric, or dangerous?

"Oh, no. Brat is carried to the park on Forsythe Street in a carrier, then let loose in a fenced area."

"I see."

"But why don't we act as if he is here," Montag suggested. "Just go into the other room and make yourself comfortable until he gets back. And I'll start to work."

Why not? I thought. I got up and walked toward the open part of the sliding partition.

"By the way, Miss Nestleton, I'd appreciate it if as part of your responsibility you answer the phone and doorbells while you're here."

"Fine. Is there an extension?"

"Yes."

I walked inside. The air was even cooler in this part of the loft. And there was a large, very comfortable easy chair with a standing light right beside it. I sat down, luxuriating in the coolness, and began to read a James tale called "The Altar of the Day."

After the first page, I kicked off my shoes. My feet were still not visible for the simple fact that I was wearing my long Virginia Woolf summer dress—a dull white flax affair that made me look like a lissome, ghostly wraith of indeterminate age stalking the downtown streets.

Time passed. The cat did not return. I put the book down. I heard the man working. I began to get more and more anxious.

What if there was no cat? What if this whole thing

was a set-up? A way to lure me there? Why? Rape? Murder? Who knew?

At nine o'clock I resolved to just walk out fast. And then, the buzzer rang.

Montag called in: "That must be Brat. Could you get him?"

I was greatly relieved.

I walked to the door, fumbled with the latch for a bit, and then swung it open. I saw something yellow.

And then I felt a terrible pain on the side of my head.

And then—well, just blankness. I was no longer there.

Sometime later, I opened my eyes. I realized I was lying on the floor, half in and half out of the open doorway.

My vision was going in and out of focus. The front of my dress was soaked. I didn't know whether it was blood or spittle or vomit.

I couldn't see a cat.

However, I could see Mr. Montag. His hands were tied behind his back. A rope was embedded in his neck. He was swinging from a light fixture, back and forth, like a metronome. But then he faded to black.